Essences of Living

A Short Story Collection

By

Nicholas O'Hare

GW00482589

Harkaway
Ireland

ISBN 0-9541310-9-6

Cover Illustration by John Ryan, Bective, Co Meath

Other books by Nicholas O'Hare

Fiction:
The Irish Secret Agent
A Spy in Dublin
The Ballylally Races
Unlawful Secrets
The Boyle Inheritance

Equestrian:

King of Diamonds
The Modern Irish Draught
The Irish Sport Horse
The Modern Connemara

Printed and bound by Antony Rowe Ltd, Eastbourne

Essences of Living

Contents

About the author

Nicholas O'Hare has a background in journalism, publishing and the Irish horse industry. He has written several novels and four equine books devoted to horsebreeding and production. In his journalistic and publishing career he edited and produced magazines and annuals, and for thirty years wrote a weekly column on equine topics for *The Irish Field*, Ireland's weekly equestrian newspaper He founded and edited the *Irish Draught Horse Yearbook* and also produced the *Irish Showjumping Annual* for a number of years

His literary pursuits have included many short stories. He was one of the earlier writers published in the New Irish Writing Page in the *Irish Press* newspaper which was edited by David Marcus.

Publishing and journalism were complemented for over forty years with an interest in horse breeding. He ran a riding school in Dublin and stood Sport Horse and Connemara pony stallions. He was an accomplished showman and won many prizes with harness ponies at Dublin Spring and Horse Shows and other venues throughout the country. His equine books have been recognized for their professionalism and knowledge of breeding and the horse industry generally and have been sold all over the world.

Since his retirement Nicholas O'Hare has devoted himself to writing. This collection of short stories is his latest literary venture .

Commitment

"How long have you been married?"

They sat across the table from Doctor Gantley. Both of them were nervous, Conor was also sullen and it showed in his stony face and petulant mouth. Imelda considered the question, carefully. It seemed innocuous enough

"Five years" she answered since it seemed that Conor was determined to say as little as possible.

He didn't want to be here. He had resisted her suggestion for as long as possible and argued about it every evening for weeks.

Imelda, however, was determined. They had been trying for a baby ever since they were married. Nothing had happened and now it was time for them to do something positive about it.

"How old are you, Mrs McArdle.

Imelda pursed her lips. The passing of the years was the engine which had driven her to this moment.

"Forty one," she answered quickly. "We were late getting married I suppose, but my life, our lives," she corrected swiftly, determined that Conor was going to remain a part of the proceedings, "were busy. We had known each other for years, but we never actually got around to tying the knot until then."

Dr Gantley nodded understandingly.

"And you've been actively trying to get pregnant for how long."

Imelda was silent for a moment. She knew that Conor resented this intrusion into their private affairs.

"From the beginning, she answered swiftly. "I – we –" She corrected herself again. "We wanted to have a family. It was the real reason why we got married," she admitted. "Otherwise our lives could have continued the way were."

Dr Gantley nodded again. He understood the situation only too well. A strict moralist, he disapproved of the current attitude to sex and marriage. The women, he felt were willing enough, but the men were careless, not too keen, anxious to avoid commitment. People moved in together, living for the moment, without any real thought of what lay ahead. Anxious old age, the threat of being alone, sickness which required companionship and assistance, all the tribulations of life. These things called for a special bonding. People didn't understand what it was really about, he mused. Co-habitation was a momentary solution, not a long term answer.

He interrupted his thoughts and brought himself back to the present. They were a likeable enough couple, he decided. The woman was worried, time was ticking away for her. The husband was resistant, slightly aggressive even. He resented this probing into matters which he considered private and personal. Dr Gantley understood only too well the emotions that were besetting Conor McArdle. He blamed his wife for their continued failure to have a child. He was certain that it was nothing to do with him as a man and he resented the fact that he had been made to expose his beliefs in this analysis of the situation by an outsider.

The doctor knew from experience that Conor McArdle would resist his efforts to assign blame. He would be unco-operative, perhaps even refuse to have the tests, firmly committed to the view that no fault could be laid at his door. Many men adopted this stance. They resented anything which might be construed as a reflection on their manhood. Any suggestion that they

6

might have problems was a slur too far.

Gantley carefully considered his next few words. It was important to minimize any possibility of insult, to compromise as far as possible but at the same time allow reality to break into the consciousness of each of the couple opposite.

"Infertility," he said carefully, "can be broken down into three sources. In one third of cases it is the fault of the female, one third the fault of the male and the final third it is the fault of both parties."

He cleared his throat and felt his way forward.

"For males sperm count is the issue. For the female there are often ovulation disorders or sometimes physical problems, generally blocked fallopian tubes. Most people seek help after a full year of ineffective intercourse. You have left things a little bit late," he went on conversationally, looking directly at Imelda.

"Your age could be an issue, and there is also a question of your nutritional balance," he went on. "Most cases can be treated with drug therapy. Sometimes improvements in nutrition can bring about a result. A course of vitamins or supplements can work wonders."

"The problem is not insurmountable," he said expansively. "I am sure that we can sort something out, but of course, as I said before, your age could be a factor."

Conor spoke up. "The drugs," he said. How long will it take them to work."

Gantley looked at him guardedly. He was making assumptions too quickly.

7

"We will have to run some tests" he said. "And I will have to carry out an internal examination of your wife. Until these matters are dealt with we cannot decide on a way forward."

Conor straightened in his chair. His face flushed angrily for a few seconds. He knew what Gantley was saying. There had to be a decision on which of them was at fault. Until the tests were concluded things were up in the air. Conor was vulnerable until then. He could well be the cause of the problem. He would not willingly submit to the tests. There was no doubt in his mind. He couldn't be firing blanks. The fault lay with Imelda. She and the doctor would have to accept this.

Imelda could read his thoughts. She interpreted his silence exactly. Conor was selfishly reviewing his options and had come to a decision. His wife was the problem. There was no more to be said. She decided to end Conor's silent self assessment.

"When can I be examined?" she asked.

Gantley looked at his watch.

"Not today" he said. "Our time together has run out. But I can make an appointment for you later in the week. We'll run some blood tests and I'll do the internal examination at the same appointment. If you can come in on Thursday morning we will get through things fairly quickly."

He decided for the moment not to press Conor for a sperm count. The situation might be easier if he dealt with the woman first. If his wife was in the clear, then Conor would have to submit without any further argument. Gantley knew that there could be difficulties ahead. He had encountered quite a number of cases where the woman was blameless and the husband still refused to recognize that fault lay with him.

COMMITMENT

He sighed. Human relationships were complex and none more so when it came to marriage and sexual issues.

They went home in subdued frames of minds. Imelda was relieved to some extent that they had at last decided on concrete action. In a way she was sorry that she had not gone ahead without Conor's knowledge. She had decided that both of them should be involved for the very good reason that it might be necessary to Conor to take stock of himself. If they both participated in the procedures, the blow for Conor, if in fact the problem was his, might not be so hard to bear. Conor was uncharacteristically silent and morose over the next few days. Imelda was uncomplaining. She knew how difficult it was for him to come to terms with the issues which they both confronted. Women were more practical, she reflected. They understood the intricacies of conception and child birth. Men played a very limited part in the process and for that reason had a very limited understanding of the pressures which a woman must carry.

Imelda went back to Dr Gantley's surgery for her blood tests and internal examination in a lighter frame of mind. The fact that she was facing up to the issue brought its own sense of relief although there was the underlying anxiety that something had to be wrong. Once or twice over the years since they were married she had believed herself to be pregnant but each time it was a false alarm. Imelda had known for nearly two years that there was a problem but Conor's refusal to become involved had created a barrier towards seeking a solution.

"There's nothing physically wrong," Dr Gantley reassured her when he had completed the examination. "We'll see what the blood tests produce but you seem to me to be in good health. If the bloods throw up some deficiency I will put you on a vitamin regime. If that doesn't work we'll consider a course of drug therapy."

"Drugs are successful in eighty five per cent of cases," he reassured her, catching the anxious look which flashed across her face. Imelda had an aversion to any kind of medication and took even cold remedies with a strong sense of reluctance.

The drugs didn't work. Five months later, Dr Gantley confessed himself beaten.

Imelda sat disconsolately in her usual chair. Conor had refused to come with her. The subject had only been briefly discussed at home. Imelda accepted that her husband didn't want to know the details. She believed that he wanted a child as much as she did, and comforted herself with the thought that if she succeeded in getting her engine running he would be quite amenable to the pressures which pregnancy would bring. Imelda really wanted to have at least two children but she realized that this was something which was unlikely to occur. If they got one child out of the maelstrom she would have to be content.

A child, she was certain, would refresh their marriage and would create a new spirit of unity. The failure to conceive had been divisive. There were strains there which were growing more and more intrusive. At least that was what Imelda believed. A chasm had been created in their lives. She never considered for one moment that Conor was uneasy in their alliance for other reasons. She was certain that there was no question of another woman. Conor's dissatisfaction, she convinced herself, arose totally from the fact that they were childless.

"What do we do now?" she asked tonelessly.

Dr Gantley adopted a professional air of cheerfulness.

"We are not at the end of the road," he said reassuringly. There's always IVF."

COMMITMENT

Imelda looked him full in the face.

"I don't know what is involved," she said. "My husband and I have never considered anything other than the natural way."

The doctor was silent for a moment or two. He realized that he was treading on delicate ground. He might be urging a course of action on his client that she might consider offensive. He didn't know what Imelda's views on invasive procedures might be but the likelihood was that she was conservative, inhibited by a natural reluctance to become involved in anything that might be construed as artificial. Religion was a smothering influence on many modern procedures. People didn't want to participate because of the feelings of guilt that they might have to carry afterwards. There was always the underlying problem that advances in medical procedures very often clashed with religious teaching.

"The procedure is relatively simple," he said. In Vitro Fertilisation has been around since 1978. I will remove your eggs from your ovary, mixed them with your husband's sperm. It will take forty hours to fertilise them. and then I will place them directly in your uterus. It's a simple procedure," he said again, looking intently at Imelda to satisfy himself that she understood.

Imelda reviewed what he had said. She had no problem with what was being proposed, but how would Conor react. There was the physical issue of securing his sperm. He was shy about himself and she was certain that he would have difficulty with complying.

"This is the only way left to us now" she asked.

The doctor was silent for a moment.

11

"We could continue with the drug therapy," he said. "But I don't think there is much point. If you want to proceed to have a child then IVF is the only alternative."

She went home in a turbulent stage of mind. She knew that she would have difficulty with Conor, but she was determined. Their marriage, their future, depended on this birth. She would have to overcome Conor's scruples his fastidiousness with anything to do with sex.

She won the argument eventually. Conor complied, resentfully and sullenly and the fertilised eggs were placed in her uterus. Pregnany followed. Imelda was ecstatic. Conor too seemed pleased although he was his usual undemonstrative self. Behind the wall with which he seemed to be surrounding himself more and more, Imelda thought she perceived the first glimmerings of change. He was more supportive, demonstrating in small ways the richness of the gift that she had furnished.

Imelda took every precaution throughout the following nine months, avoiding unnecessary exertion, taking the right foods, avoiding the occasional drink and cigarette which she sometimes took in moments of stress. She was determined that nothing would go wrong. They had gone through too much This baby would be the most wonderful thing that she and Conor had done together. Their marriage would have whole new dimension. Life would have a whole new meaning.

The weeks and months of the pregnancy flew by. Imelda lived them to the full. Every moment of discomfort, sickness and finally the kicks in her stomach were hallmarks of the victory that had been achieved over heir previous infertility. Imelda was now approaching her forty second birthday. The job of childbearing was overshadowed to some extent by the realization that there would be only one baby, that age would countermand any longing that she had to produce a second child. But she was content. So much had been achieved.

The birth was relatively easy. She decided to have an epidural wanting to savour every minute. Conor disappointed her. He refused to be present and spent most of the preceding day at home. She was angry with him, but refused to let this spoil what she viewed as the most important day of her life. Men were like that, she reasoned, uncaring and unfeeling at the times when concern counted most. Conor couldn't face the trauma of childbirth. He was squeamish about so many things His refusal to stay in the room for the birth was not totally unexpected, but she really felt that he could have made more of an effort. After all it was their first and only baby. Their family was going to swell with this small addition to their lives. Surely it was not too much to expect that he would have shared in the pain and joy.

She lay back when it was all over. They took the baby away for a time, but she had heard it cry and knew that it was alive. It's a boy, they told her, and a broad smile creased her face. Conor would be pleased. A son, she was certain, would overcome all the misgivings, all the reservations and objections which had made the initial stages of procreation so difficult. She was surprised that they had not given the baby to her to hold and she waited anxiously for its return. The nurses were attentive, murmuring solicitously, bringing her a drink, smoothing down the covers on the bed.

The first stirrings of alarm came when the doctor approached. A nurse walked a few paces behind him. Their faces were grave but Imelda was sure that all was well. The nurse held a small bundle in her arms, and it cried and gurgled. Her baby was alive and that was all that mattered.

They laid him down beside her and Imelda gathered up the tiny form in her arms and pressed her lips to its cheek. Then she held him up in front of her both hands securely clasped to each side. It was then that she noticed how flat his face was. His head was small, the ears tiny. The eyes were unusual. She took diminutive fingers in her own and registered that the hands were short and broad, the fingers too, she thought, were unusually short.

Sudden fear coursed through her. She looked appealingly at the doctor for an explanation.

He pulled up a bedside chair and sat down.

"There is no easy way to say this, Mrs McArdle," he said, a tinge of emotion in his voice. "Your baby has Down's Syndrome. He will need a great deal of care. We have concerns about his heart. We may have to operate."

Imelda barely heard him. She was still encased in the euphoria of giving birth. But slowly the realization of what he was saying hit her. Her baby was damaged, less than perfect. He would need love and care. Years of tribulation stretched out ahead of her. She smiled at the doctor and the nurses and clasped her son tightly to her. However imperfect this was her baby, her creation. She would assume the burden which lay ahead without demur. Her love for her baby son was total, unrestrained. She would dedicate every part of her being to him. There would be no holding back. What ever lay ahead a mother's love was absolute. She would love him for ever. She was his mother.

Scorn

Chika walked purposely from the plane. It was important that he didn't show any concern. He mingled with the rest of the passengers and followed those in front of him. Most of those ahead walked down the channel signposted EU citizens. Chika followed. The immigration officers at the foreign barrier were busy examining passports and checking in the visitors. Chika pressed on.

He was certain that his colour might have attracted attention but there were other black skins on the passenger list and no one paid him any attention. He reached the arrivals area where eager friends and relatives of the passengers waited. There was no one to welcome him. He was alone in a strange land where, he had been assured by his mother as she made a tearful goodbye in Lagos, the people were welcoming. He would be well looked after and he could start a new life. He stood for a few moments watching the carousel hum around with its cargo of luggage. He had nothing to collect. His worldly possessions were in the small suitcase that he had carried on to the airplane as hand luggage. He turned away and looked for the exit. It was important to keep moving.

Chika was sixteen. Old enough to travel to the far side of the world but young enough to want to return to his home and family. He wished that he had never set out on this journey but there was no turning back. There was nothing for him at home. No work, no further education, only the soulless descent into poverty, drinking and drugs. In Ireland, his mother had assured him, he would start a new life. He would find work, be educated, provided with food and a place to stay. The money he would send home would give his mother and his five siblings a lift from the impoverished world in which they lived.

Chika climbed into the airport bus and sat down near the back. He was still fearful that the immigration officers would suddenly realize who he was and come and seize him. But the bus filled up and the driver started the engine and they drew away from the airport complex.

A huge flashing sign at the side of the road attracted his attention. It spelled out three words in a language that Chika didn't understand.

Cead Mile Failte!

He glanced at the man sitting next to him

"It means a hundred thousand welcomes," he said in explanation. "It's Irish."

It was news to Chika that Ireland had a language. He thought everyone spoke English. He leaned back in his seat suddenly at ease. A hundred thousand welcomes! It was extravagant, but heartwarming. He was going to like Ireland.

"Go to a small town," his mother had urged him. "They will be more welcoming there. Dublin is a big city. It will be harder to settle down. There will be lots of officials and form filling. In a small place the people will be warmer and they will help you."

He looked out at the industrialised landscape that straggled along the airport road. It was a lot like Lagos, he reflected. Factories circling round the outskirts, people crammed into their homes inside the ring of warehouses and factory units that stretched out into the countryside. The traffic was heavy, he reflected, proof that this was a thriving place. Everybody had something to do and somewhere to go, always in a hurry.

The bus brought him to the central bus terminal. He followed the crowd into the foyer and stood indecisively for a few moments. There were buses waiting for passengers at pickup points on the outside of the building. Clearly there were plenty of places to go. The question was which town should he pick. His fear of capture by the immigration officials died away. There was no one here who had any authority to question him. There were plenty of uniforms around, but they were bus people all intent on carrying out their duties.

He walked over to a row of ticket offices and studied the notice boards overhead. The lists of towns meant nothing to him. The names were strange. There was no indication of how far away from Dublin they were. A man elbowed him aside anxious to get a ticket for his journey. Chika fingered the small stock of EU notes which his mother had exchanged at Lagos airport. He had seventy euros. He didn't know what a euro was worth and there was no indication of how much a bus journey would cost. He had already spent ten euros on getting from the airport to the bus terminal. He could not afford to pay out much more.

It was his turn at the counter. He scanned the list of towns overhead and picked one at random.

"To Navan," he said rapidly conscious that any hesitation or apparent unfamiliarity with the procedure would attract attention.

The clerk at the ticket counter produced a ticket and stated the fare. Eight euros. He evinced no interest in Chika at all, intent only on getting paid and tendering the correct change. Chika moved away quickly and looked at his ticket. He had a destination. He studied the signs along the glass front of the bus station and found the bay for the bus he needed. It was already waiting, about a dozen or so people on board. Again he went to the back and sat down, watchful for any sign of pursuit. There was none. No one on the bus took the slightest notice of him.

The bus slowly nosed out of the station and found its way to a carriage way which led out of the city. Chika again looked curiously out of the windows. This time there were housing estates as well as factories, and within half an hour they were in open countryside. There were few stops, the bus was an express and evidently went further than Navan, his destination. It was nearly three quarters full, country people making their way homewards, he surmised. He had the double seat to himself. There were several empty places And he settled back to doze, tired now that he had accomplished his aim of getting into the country without any hitch.

Once again he fingered the euro notes in his pocket. There were three, twenties. He had a few coins as well. He took them out. They were unfamiliar, but he estimated that he had about two euros in change. It was not much with which to start out on a new life. His mother had given him all that she could spare, determined to give the best chance she could. Someday soon, he promised himself, he would repay her. When he had a job he would send money home every week.

The journey was relatively brief. Less than thirty kilometres he estimated. It had taken about an hour. He got out and found himself in a narrow shop lined street. There were plenty of people walking the footpaths. It seemed a busy place. The traffic was one way. He crossed to an awning fronted café and ordered a cup of coffee. Although the charge was small it made further inroads into his limited store of cash which he could ill afford. But he was tired and thirsty. The coffee would refresh him. He had a lot yet to do. The first thing on the agenda was to find a place to stay. This was what his mother had told him. Get an address, a base. Then contact the authorities and register as an asylum seeker.

He lingered over his coffee, wanting to postpone the inevitable effort and complexity of negotiating for a room. It had been a long stay since the early morning flight from Lagos airport to

Paris, and then on to Dublin. He was going to Ireland on holiday, he told a bored French official who waved him through to his change of airplane without any verbal contact whatsoever. It had been easy, he told himself. Far easier indeed than traveling around at home, where there was a constant need to get through police checks and roadblocks.

The waitress asked him did he want anything else and he realized that he was in danger of overstaying his welcome. A cup of coffee only bought so much sitting down time. He looked at his watch and realized that he had been there for over an hour. He must not make that mistake again, he told himself. That sort of carelessness could arouse suspicion. It was an automatic caution. Here quite clearly there were no probing police eyes, no touts on the lookout for victims whom they could denounce to the authorities. Nonetheless he must be cautious. He was a stranger, a black face amongst the white. Only when he had been granted the coveted refugee status could he relax and behave in a normal way.

He went out into the street again and walked downhill towards a church. The Irish were very religious, he knew. He himself was a member of the United Church of God on the outskirts of Lagos. All the family were members and went every Sunday, singing along with gusto when the hymns were called by an exuberant Pastor Ade Unyolo, listening avidly to thundering sermons and exhortations to avoid sins. But was life in Nigeria not in itself a sin. Poverty was universal. A small class of relatively super rich governing the thousands upon thousands of people who lived in shanty towns with those who were fortunate enough eking out a precarious living in low paid menial jobs.

He left the shopping area behind and walked along a street which was lined with private houses, some in terraces, others standing in double fronted superiority. He halted at one of these. It was a newly painted residence with flower boxes on the windowsills. A hanging sign announced bed and breakfast. There was a tourist organization logo on the wall as well. He knocked and after a moment or two heard footsteps. A grey haired woman in her middle fifties open the door and looked expectantly at her visitor.

If the landlady was bothered about his colour she gave no sign. He was brought in, offered the register to sign, and led upstairs to a cheerful room at the back of the house. The tariff was twenty euros a night, she told him. Chika said he would stay one night. He brought out his sparse supply of euro notes and offered her a twenty. She waved it aside.

"It will do in the morning," she said. "You might want to stay for more than one night."

Chika agreed with her. He might indeed. But that was dependant on his getting rapid assistance from the authorities. He had cash for three nights board, no more, but it was important that he had an address. His mother had told him this.

"They will send you to a centre if you don't" she had said. "But if you have an address they will pay to keep you there. It's better that you should live privately."

The landlady left and he put his suitcase on the bed. It contained a second pair of jeans, a sweater, and some changes of underwear and socks. He had traveled light. Indeed he had no option. Material possessions were scarce in Chika's world.

Chika stayed in his room for the rest of the day, dozing fitfully and rehearsing his story for delivery to the authorities. The landlady brought him a cup of tea and biscuits, apologizing for the fact that she couldn't serve an evening meal. Chika smiled his thanks. He warmed to this motherly conscientious woman who was clearly so keen to look after him.

SCORN

He walked the streets of the town the following morning trying to pluck up courage to go into the police station and report himself. He went to within a few yards of the grim grey building, but somehow its vaguely forbidding aspect reminded him of the police stations at home. There people stayed away from the police. Here he had to make himself known and submit to whatever process they involved him in. Were policemen not the same the world over, he asked himself. Was there really that much difference between the Irish police and the harsh security minded corps which subdued his own country.

He wandered around the shops, went to the main shopping center and spent a couple of euros on a sparse meal in the cafeteria. His money was slowly trickling away. Now he had eaten into the three night's rent which he had been hoarding. He would only be able to pay for two nights now, but still the urgency of his situation was not strong enough to overcome his reluctance to turn himself in to the authorities. He bought a newspaper and idly scanned the headlines. The news meant nothing to him. He knew nothing of this country in which he had elected to seek his future. His English was good, his mother had made sure that he went to school every day, and he could read better than he spoke, but after a few minutes he put down the newspaper.

He left the cafeteria and went back to roaming the streets. There were other black faces in the town. Not that many Africans, but quite a few Indians, the women in the ground trailing dresses which they wore at home, and quite a few Filipinos and Chinese. Navan seemed to be a cosmopolitan place. He wondered if all Irish towns were like this, infiltrated with nationalities from around the world. The thought raised his spirits. Clearly it was relatively easy to be accepted as a refugee.

21

Finally he plucked up courage and walked back to the police station. After a moment or two of hesitation outside he went in and spoke to the officer on duty at the public counter.

The policeman heard him out and produced a form. He didn't give it to Chika but wrote down his responses to a list of questions. Chika told him his name, spelled it out, A-d-u-b-u, to make sure that it was written down correctly. He gave the boarding house as his address and told the officer his age.

"Sixteen," the other echoed tonelessly. "You're under age then. Unaccompanied. Did you come here on your own?"

Chika nodded affirmatively.

"You'll have to go to the Health Board," the policeman said. "They look after minors."

"I want to claim asylum," Chika insisted, feeling somehow that control of events was slipping away from him. The Health Board didn't sound right.

"They'll look after that," the policeman responded.

He lifted a phone and dialed a number. A few moments conversation ensued and he scribbled down an address on a piece of paper. He gave some directions which Chika found confusing and motioned the boy to be gone. The interview was over.

Chika went outside and scrutinised the scrap of paper.

The writing was scrawled and meant nothing to him. He stopped a passerby and proffered the slip. The man pointed down the street and gestured his directions. Chika found his accent difficult to understand but went in the direction indicated. Finally after several inquiries from people in the street he located the Health Board office.

He went inside and told the girl at the counter his situation. It was almost word for word the story that he had told the policeman. She listened and when he had finished went to an inside office. Another woman, older this time, emerged complete with several sheets of paper. More forms, more questions, Chika thought, impatient at the failure to get to grips with his affairs.

The usual questions followed. The woman queried his age and frowned when he insisted that he was only sixteen. He showed her his passport to confirm that he was telling the truth.

"Very well," she said resignedly. "I suppose we'll have to look after you."

"I need help to pay for my accommodation" Chika said. "There is a scheme for paying refugees?"

She frowned again.

"This country looks after your sort of people well," she said. "But you're under age. You'll have to stay in a hostel."

"I have an address," Chika protested. He was certain that his bed and breakfast room would be preferable to dormitory accommodation in a Health Board hostel.

"You have to stay where we send you," the woman said. "You have to be looked after. "You're under age," she said again."

Then struck by another line of thought she began to question him about his entry to the country.

"I flew in from Lagos," Chika responded.

The woman frowned once more.

"You should have reported to the immigration authorities at the airport," she said. "You're not supposed to go around the country on your own."

Chika said nothing.

"I'll send your forms to Dublin,' the woman said eventually. "They'll come to a decision about you."

"I'm a refugee" Chika re-emphasised.

"Of course you are," the woman commented. "I understand that. Come back in a week's time and we'll have some news for you"

"I need money to pay my lodgings,' Chika said. "Stay there for the moment," the woman replied. "We'll organize a weekly payment for you."

"I want to get a job as soon as possible," Chika said.

"Oh you're not allowed to work," the woman responded sharply. "You're a refugee. You can't work. We don't allow it. You'll get your rent and food paid for, and you'll be given a spending allowance. When the paper work is completed," she promised.

Chika was concerned.

"I have very little money left," he said.

"What am I to do?"

The woman pursed her lips.

"You'll get an allowance in due course," she said. There is a procedure to be gone through. You should have reported at the airport. It takes longer here."

She was silent for a moment or two.

"You can't work," she said again. "But you can go to school. You'll have to get into a course," she went on. "That's what people your age do. They get on a course and continue with their education."

It was Chika's turn to be silent. He had set his mind on getting a job. Not being allowed to work was disconcerting. His family needed the money. He had promised them. He would send home whatever he could spare from his wages. No work meant no money for his mother. It was ridiculous, he thought. Everyone was entitled to work.

"Come back next week," the woman urged. "Everything will have been sorted out by then."

"I don't have enough money to pay for my lodgings for that long," Chika said.

The woman was getting impatient.

"Just stay at that address," she said. "The Welfare officer will call around. He'll give you some money to tide you over."

He went back to the B and B. The landlady met him in the hall.

"Do you know how long you will be staying yet" she asked. "I don't want to let your room if you're staying on."

"I've been told to stay here until I'm contacted" he said. "The Welfare officer will be calling to give me some money."

"The Welfare officer" she repeated. A look of annoyance crossed her face. "Are you unemployed. I thought you were working at the hospital. We don't take in social welfare people here."

She was clearly annoyed.

Chika tried to soothe her.

"The Health Board are going to give me money," he said. "They'll pay for my accommodation. They told me to stay here until I am contacted."

"I'm not interested," the woman spat out. "I don't want your sort here. It will be months before I get any money and I'll have to buy you food and be at the loss of my income in the mean time."

Chika didn't know what to say. The landlady was so obviously hostile.

"I'm sorry" he said apologetically. "I didn't realize that I would be a problem."

"The country is overrun with your sort," she went on angrily. "Spongers. Coming here to live off our social services. We don't pay our taxes to support the likes of you. You should be stopped coming here. You should stay in your own country."

"I'm an asylum seeker," he said in a half hearted attempt to regain his position. "I couldn't stay at home. My family are poor and I would have to go into the army. I hope to make a new life here. I will get a job and send money home to my mother."

Slightly mollified at this recitation of his good intentions, she adopted a less combatant tone.

26

SCORN

"You had money when you came," she said. "What have you done with that."

He took out his wallet and extracted his depleted wad of two blue twenty euro notes.

She snatched them out of his hand.

"This will pay for two days," she said sharply. "After that you'll have to go. I'm not running an account with the Health Board. I like my money in my hand. That's how I do business. People pay when they stay here"

She turned and walked angrily into the kitchen at the back of the house. Chika went disconsolately to his room and lay down on the bred. He put his hands in his trousers pocket and extracted the few coins he had left. Seven euros. The altercation with the landlady coming on top of his dealings with the police and the Health Board people had upset him. Suddenly he was lonely. Ireland didn't seem as welcoming after all.

He stayed in his room for a couple of hours and then bored with his surroundings went out. He walked to the outskirts of the town and noticed a group of around his own age congregated outside a supermarket. Most of them were boys but there were some girls as well. He joined them. At first they were curious about him, asking his name, where he was from, but then after several minutes they all moved off.

Chika followed. He needed companionship. These young people offered a first glimpse of a more sociable Irish lifestyle. Inside he hankered for his own comrades back home in Lagos. Devastatingly poor, without prospects, they nonetheless had an innate sense of optimism. These young people were the same. They were white, of course, but then nearly everyone in Ireland was white. Coming from a black township, Chika had

27

never experienced racial prejudice. The white people in Nigeria now had so little power as to be of no consequence. It was the black rulers with their troops, their militias, and their cane wielding police who were to be feared and despised.

At first the group took no notice of him. Chika thought that he had been accepted and his spirits rose. Then one of the ringleaders turned on him and demanded to know what he was doing following them.

"Clear off," he shouted at Chika. It wasn't the word clear that he used. Chika surmised it was a swear word but he read its meaning well enough. The others gathered round jeering.

"Black bastard,' one of them shouted. "Nigger," screamed another."

They were hostile now, menacing. Chika wasn't too alarmed. He was used to rough and tumble, some minor violence even, on his own streets.

"We don't want you with us," one of the girls shouted. She swore at him as well. Chika was disappointed. He had wanted to make friends with this group. He moved away a metre or two and stood there disconsolately. There was some discussion between the leading boys in the group and then one of them beckoned him closer.

"We're going to get a car," he said. "If you want to join up with us you have to drive."

Chika didn't know how to drive. No one in his family had owned a car. Several of the neighbours had beaten up trucks that they used to drive to work in, but there had been no opportunity for him to master the controls.

He told them this and there was a momentary silence.

"Alright," the leading boy said "But you've got to take part in the heist."

Chika agreed.

He wasn't sure what was coming up, but if this offered a way into acceptance by the group he was all for it.

They moved off again, an air of expectancy hanging over them. Chika worked his way into the middle of the group and walked along with rising spirits.

Finally the leaders called a halt and went into a huddle.

They were in a housing estate now. The street lights had come on and darkness was closing in.

"There's a BMW at number twenty three," one of the ringleaders said. "You and Billy go up there and get it away."

Billy was a low sized cigarette smoker slightly older than Chika. He nodded at the Nigerian youth and stubbed out his smoke. Some one produced a thin metal bar and handed it to the black boy.

"This will get the door open," he said. "Billy will do the wires."

Chika clasped the metal bar in his right hand and looked expectantly at Billy. The white boy led the way. Chika counted off the houses. They all had numbers on their doors. It was a good class estate, he decided. Nearly all of them had cars parked in their driveways, sometimes two.

Billy halted. Number twenty three was two houses up. A sleek blue BMW was parked outside, obviously fairly new, obviously valuable. Chika handed the iron bar to Billy.

"I don't know how to do this," he said.

Billy muttered something and snatched it out of Chika's hand. He walked quickly to the target car and forced the bar into the window socket. After a moment or two the door swung open. Billy slipped inside and tore at the ignition wiring underneath the dashboard. Hesitantly Chika opened the passenger side door and got in. They sat in silence while Billy did his work. Suddenly the car started. Billy grunted in satisfaction pushed the gearstick into reverse and backed rapidly on to the street. He drove down to where the group were clustered together and three or four of the boys piled into the back. Then they were off. A crazy eighty miles an hour stampede through the housing estate and out on to the main road.

They drove around for an hour or so with driving rotating amongst the passengers. Chika was exhilarated. They were driving dangerously but he didn't care. This was belonging. He had found friends. He was accepted.

The end came quickly. Billy was back at the wheel and they were screaming up a narrow roadway at nearly ninety miles an hour when traffic cones and a red light appeared ahead. Billy made no attempt to slow down. Chika knew what was going to happen. Too late Billy saw a car coming in the opposite direction. He pulled violently at the wheel to avoid it and crashed through the cones. He lost control and the car slewed into a garden hedge at the side of the road.

The hedge unquestionably saved their lives. They were in someone's front garden, the wheels carving ploughed furrows in the lawn. Chika hit his head off the windscreen and was knocked out for a moment or two. When he came round, the people from the house were at the car, his companions had vanished into the night. Chika allowed himself to be pulled out and submitted to restraining hands which both propped him up and held him at the same time.

"Joy riders" some one said. The man holding him tightened his grip.

"At least we've got one of them," he said.

A small crowd was gathering, neighbours, drawn from their television sets by the rending and tearing of the car through the hedge.

"Look at the garden," a woman spoke. "It's destroyed."

Chika tried to recapture his senses. He was dazed but apparently unhurt. His head was sore, and there was a small trickle of blood coursing down his face.

"I've rung the police," some one announced. "They'll be here in a minute. We're to hold on to this fella."

"He's one of those immigrants," the man holding him said. "Good for nothing. Coming in here and sponging off us. Thieves they are. They've destroyed this car and our garden. I wonder who owns the car. It's nearly new. Bastards."

He gave Chika a shake but the flashing blue lights of the arriving police vehicle interrupted any thoughts he might have had of further violence.

One of the policemen started to make notes, the other took hold of Chika, fitted him with plastic wrist restraints and propelled him into the back of the police car. After some ten minutes of notetaking, both officers got into the car and set off towards the town. They ignored Chika, one of them lit a cigarette.

The same officer who had interviewed Chika when he had gone into announce his presence in the country was on duty in the police station. He recognized Chika.

31

"It didn't take you long to get into trouble," he said, reaching for a form.

"What's your name again."

Chika spelled it out for him. A-d-u-b-u.

They looked at his head wound, asked him did he want a doctor. Chika said no. He wanted to cause as little trouble as possible. One of the policemen who had arrested him read out charges. Theft of a motor car, allowing himself to be carried in a stolen vehicle, malicious damage. They wanted to know who was driving, who else was in the car. Chika said nothing. The only name he had was Billy, but he wasn't going to disclose this. At home it was the same, the police were the enemy. If you were caught you said nothing. There they would beat you, but no one showed any indication of violence. It was all very matter of fact, commonplace, an incident in a night's work for urban policemen who encountered violence and vandalism on every shift.

They put him in a cell and gave him a cup of tea later on. Chika lay down on the bunk and tried to ease his throbbing head. He could have done with an aspirin but he wouldn't ask for one. The less contact he had the better.

They brought him to court the following morning. The arresting officer gave evidence. Chika pleaded guilty to the charges. There was no point in doing anything else. He had been caught in the wreckage of a stolen car. The police officer elaborated on his background.

"He's a refugee," he told the judge. "Arrived here two days ago. He has no status yet. Some paper work has been done, but nothing has been determined."

SCORN

The judge looked down distastefully at Chika. He wore a black robe and heavy black rimmed spectacles. He was clearly not impressed.

"You have two choices," he said to Chika. "You can go to jail for two years or you can go back to your own country. Which is it to be?"

Chika thought rapidly. He didn't want to go to jail in this foreign country where he knew no one. To be sent home in disgrace was not really an option either. His mother would be heartbroken after all the effort she had made to save the money to get him to Ireland"

He spoke up dispiritedly.

"I'll go home," he said.

The judge nodded. He looked at the policeman in the witness box.

"See to it. As soon as possible. We don't want his sort here and we certainly don't want to spend a lot of money looking after him."

The policeman left the witness box and took Chika by the arm. The restraints were put on again. He was brought back to the police station and put into a cell once more. Five or six hours passed and a different officer came into the cell. He was accompanied by a second man in civilian clothes.

"I'm from the National Immigration Bureau" he said to Chika. "We're taking you to the airport. There's a charter flight to Lagos tonight. You'll be on it. There's a few more of your sort going out as well."

Within half an hour he was in the back of a car once more

heading for Dublin Airport. There were three policemen in the car, all of them in civilian clothes. It was dark. He looked at his watch, bought cheaply in the market in Lagos. Just after eleven o'clock.

"The plane goes out at midnight," the officer beside him said, capturing Chika's glimpse at his watch. "You'll be amongst friends. There are twenty other Nigerians going with you. We're getting rid of your sort as quickly as we can."

Chika said nothing. He stared miserably at the lights of the housing estates and industrial units as they passed. The great adventure was over. The chance for a better life destroyed. He had let everyone down. The future held nothing other than a worthless, workless empty life, tempered perhaps with bouts of drinking with his neighbours who would share his misfortune. It was the way things were in Lagos. Ireland had at first held out a different promise.

They passed the big flashing sign which he had seen on the way in from the airport. Its message was unchanged. He remembered the translation. A hundred thousand welcomes! His mouth curled in derision, scorn. Ireland had not given him a single welcome never mind a hundred thousand.

Ambition

An Olympic gold for Ireland! It was a dream come true. Martin shared in the exultation of every Irish horseman at the great victory in Athens. Like thousands of young people all over the country he was spurred to make his own mark on Irish showjumping. Where one rider could go surely others could follow. Every Irish youngster who had a horse was inspired. They too would be achievers. They too would win gold medals for Ireland.

Martin went down to the riding school whenever he had free time. There were classes, of course, on weekdays, but his mother raised no objection when he was finished up at school and went down to see the horses before it got dark. At weekends there were no restrictions. Saturdays and Sundays were long carefree days when the smell of hay and horses could be savoured to the maximum.

The riding school was close to home barely three quarters of a mile away. His mother brought him down in the car and picked him up when she judged he had spent long enough out of her sight. Martin's dreams were of horses and more horses, of riding and winning, of jumping the big tracks in the Main Arena at Dublin Horse Show, of waving at the cheering crowds applauding a famous victory by Martin Lynch on his wonder horse.

For Martin had a wonder horse This was the eleven years old Mustard who worked in the riding school. He was the horse of his dreams. There was no horse like Mustard, the boy affirmed. He was easy, child and adult were safe on his back, and he was a jumper. Martin had a keen eye honed by years of careful scrutiny of all the horses in the yard. He knew which of the horses had potential, which were nervous and stroppy, which were safe to go behind.

'Take care' was the lesson which had been drummed into

Martin from an early age by his parents and by Helen and the girls who worked in the riding school. Horses were large animals which had to be treated with respect. You were careful around them and did not get into situations which were likely to bring about trouble. Martin learned well. He knew which horses he could approach, the tails which he could brush out, the legs which he could rub down when they were wet or muddy. There were horses he could get close to and others which might swing their quarters around or stamp agitatedly while they were being groomed. Some might snap peevishly, resentful of the scraping of the brushes. Others were content to stand and let their bodies be caressed.

Mustard had been Martin's favourite for as long as he could remember. They called him Mustard because of his bright dun coat not for any extreme of temperament which could cause him to be classified as hot. Sometimes Martin wished that Mustard would show a little more spark. He was almost too laid back on the lessons, hopping over the small jumps and cantering easily through the corners of the arena with indifferent riders pulling at his mouth.

But Mustard had hidden talents. He deserved a better life than working in a riding school. Martin had been around when a special rider had come to the yard one day and given him a school over the fences in the paddock. Mustard had excelled himself under this experienced educated horseman. The stable girls had put up the fences to showjumping height and he had sailed out over them without hesitation and without knocking a pole. Martin watched and marveled. He longed to be as good a rider as the visitor. Surely Mustard could go on to greater things.

The stranger had come looking for a horse to buy. Martin had no fears that he would take Mustard away. He had a problem with his wind and wouldn't pass the vet. Everyone had a horse examined before they parted with any cash. Mustard had been examined before and failed. Martin had asked his uncle who was a knowledgeable man about horses if Mustard's wind would keep from becoming a top class showjumper. His uncle had shaken his head and said no. A showjumping horse didn't need to be as clean in the wind as a racehorse. Many top showjumpers made a noise as they went around the arenas. It wasn't a good thing in a horse but if they could jump well enough it didn't affect their value. But Martin knew that professional would be customers wanted sound horses unless, of course, they were special in other ways. He had no fears that Mustard would be bought by this man and leave the yard. He knew too much and was too particular, Martin decided. He wouldn't need the vet to tell him that Mustard had faulty wind. He could hear it for himself and because he wanted a horse which he could sell on, he would leave Mustard where he was and look for something else.

As Martin had expected there was no sale. Mustard had ridden well enough and jumped spectacularly but the would be buyer couldn't take any chances. When he went to sell again the wind problem might come against him and he would lose his profit. Anyway he wanted a hunter and a hunter had to gallop. His wind had to be right for that. The day might come, Martin knew, when someone would ignore his wind problem and try to take Mustard away. It might be sooner rather than later. The advertisment offering him for sale was in the newspapers. There would be other buyers, someone perhaps who would ignore Mustard's wind problem, but take him away, not for glittering future as a showjumper, but perhaps to work in another riding school, perhaps as a riding horse in a private yard, perhaps to put him on the boat for England.

Martin could not afford to delay any longer. Mustard must come to him. He wasn't quite ready. He had money saved up, but not enough. He was certain that he could persuade his father to make up the difference. It would take a lot of persuasion but there was no way that he would let Mustard fall into other hands. Martin had his dream. Mustard's destiny was to jump for Ireland.

Helen decided to boost the chance of a sale for Mustard by taking him to a show. Helen had been a competition rider before she set up the riding school and still went jumping when time allowed. Martin was concerned. He knew that showjumping people would be quick to spot Mustard's potential if he showed any promise at all. He persuaded his father to bring him to the show, anxious to keep track of events. If there was anyone on hand to make a bid for Mustard, Martin would be around to hear of it.

Horses, he knew were not sold instantly. There had to be time for assessment, particularly of showjumpers, and offers had to be mulled over. But he knew that Helen needed cash and that she was anxious for a quick sale. If he jumped well enough no one here would care about him making a noise. Ability governed the buying and selling of showjumping horses. That was what it was all about. Mustard was a horse with a jump. In the right hands he could go a long way.

Mustard was entered in the novice class. Showjumping competitions were graded with horses being eligible by the number of points they had won. Martin knew that Mustard would have no difficulty in getting a clear round at this level. And so it proved. He sailed around the course clearing every fence. Martin was alternately exuberant and concerned. He was elated by the fact that Mustard had done so well, concerned by the possibility that someone would want to buy him. He was a physical as well as a performing attraction. His yellow dun coat gleamed in the sunshine and as he leaped over the obstacles Martin could see that he was an eye catcher.

Several horses had clear rounds and there would be a jump off, this time against the clock. These days a horse had to be a really good performer to capture a red rosette in a showjumping competition. The days when four faults was an acceptable score were long gone. There were too many horses with ability on the circuit. A clear round had to be achieved. But it was a clear round which had brought the young Irish rider Olympic gold at Athens. That was the standard. Martin had no doubt that Mustard could fight his way to the top. All he needed was experience and opportunity.

Helen went out for her second round and Martin watched expectantly at the ringside. Mustard rolled a pole at the third fence, but it stayed in place and no faults were incurred. There were ten fences to be jumped and as he set himself for every obstacle Martin prayed that he would clear each one. And indeed he did. Mustard was a true performer, an honest horse who tried his best at every fence. There were admiring comments from the people around him, one or two remarked on his wind, but in their eyes it was not a fault. Mustard was a jumper and these jumping people gave him credit for every fence.

Helen divided first place with another rider and came smiling out of the ring after the presentation of the rosettes. Mustard would get points for his performance as well and he had been given a start up the competitive ladder. If he kept this up it would not be long before he was upgraded and jumping with the more experienced horses. But Martin knew that Helen wasn't interested in campaigning Mustard around the showjumping tracks. She wanted to sell him. The need for money overrode all other considerations. Even as she came out of the ring she was looking around for possible buyers. If there was anyone at the show who had an interest this was the time when they would make their move.

Martin watched closely as Helen slipped out of the saddle. Almost immediately she was approached by a tall thin man that Martin knew by repute. He was Ruben Bowden, a leading

39

horse dealer who specialised in buying horses for export. He was based in Wales but was a familiar figure at the Irish shows. He was known to be a committed supporter of Irish horses and a valuable customer but known also for the fact that his prices had a limit. Not for him the extravagant sums often offered by American or Arab customers. Bowden was a shrewd businessman, knew what he wanted, but drove a hard bargain. Helen wouldn't get a fortune for Mustard from him, but he was a payer and would write a cheque for the horse there and then.

Alarmed at Bowden's approach to Helen, Martin knew that it was time to strike. He took his father by the arm and looked at him earnestly.

"I want to buy Mustard," he said. "We have to do it now. You'll have to help me. We'll lose him if we don't do something right away."

There was an urgency in Martin's voice that his father could not resist. He knew that sooner or later he would have to buy a horse for Martin. It was his son's main ambition, he longed to be an owner of a horse with prospects. Martin had been saving up for months. Donal Lynch knew that he would have to put money, perhaps a large enough sum, to his son's savings, but he knew also that the day had come when Martin could not be denied.

All his life Martin had been a horse fanatic. His obsession and his daily pilgrimages to the riding stables had at first given his parents some concern. They would have liked Martin to have some other interests, but they realised that horses meant something special to their son. He bought all the magazines, went to as many shows as he could, and put away all his spare money towards the day when he would buy and own a horse. Donal Lynch knew instinctively that the day had come. Martin had always been a fan of Mustard, talked about him incessantly at mealtimes, and would be heart broken if he slipped away from him.

Martin pointed across the showgrounds to Helen and the dealer. They made their way towards them. Helen was deep in conversation with the buyer, but broke off when Martin and his father approached.

Donal Lynch wasted no time in getting to the point. He would do anything for his son, make any sacrifice. Martin's enthusiasm and commitment were infectious. His son made few demands on his parents. He had worked well at school, and the time had come for decisions to be made about his future. That horses would be a part of that future was a an issue for debate and concern. Both mother and father knew that there were problems ahead. Donal Lynch knew that Martin's mind was made up. There was little else on the horizon. Martin strained so hard to be an owner, to belong to the horse world, to play his part. For Donal there was no other option. His son was making his first demand on him as a father. He wanted this horse and Donal was determined that he should have him.

"We want to buy Mustard, " he said immediately. "Martin has made up his mind."

Ruben Bowen laughed good humouredly.

"That gives you two customers," he said to Helen. "You're in luck today."

Helen was startled. She hadn't expected Martin and his father's approach.

"I was about to do a deal with Ruben," she said. "I don't know what to say."

41

"I'll top any other offer you get," Donal Lynch said. "It's important to us. Martin has been saving up and I will put up the rest of the money."

Helen looked doubtful. Ruben Bowden looked speculatively at father and son.

"Owning a horse is a big responsibility," he said. "There's quite a lot involved. Are you sure that you want this particular horse."

Martin spoke up.

"I know Mustard is a good horse," he said. "That's why I want him. I don't just want to own any old horse. Mustard is the horse for me. I've had my eye on him for a long time.

"That's true enough," Helen said. "You're always around him in the yard. But there are other horses. Ruben was going to give me a good price."

"We'll top it" Donal Lynch said again, the challenge posed by the dealer stimulating an adversarial streak in his make up. He would be as good a man as Ruben Bowden. His son wanted this horse. He would see that he got it.

But Bowden was not a man to be easily defeated. A lifetime of horse dealing and coping with horse lovers had honed his skills. He was a tough man but he knew that horses had a special impact on all those who came in contact with them. He understood Martin's ambition. He too had been a boy once and had hankered for his first horse which to him had also seemed out of reach. Ruben Bowden had made a success out of his calling by keeping sentiment in check and conducting his transactions on the basis that he had to get value for everything he spent. But he understood Martin's motivation. He understood it but he would overcome it nonetheless.

42

AMBITION

It was not often that he encountered opposition. Sometimes people bid against him at auctions and he often had to give way with good grace, but when it came to private deals Bowden was seldom found wanting. He knew his horseflesh and he knew to the last what he could get for a horse when he came to sell him on again. This golden dun Irish horse was something special and he was determined that a man and a boy driven by sentiment would not get the better of him.

Ruben quietly weighed up his opposition. He was certain that he could outbid them. There had to be a limit to the amount of money that these people could put up. They weren't professional horse people. The boy was keen and clearly had picked up a lot from his time around the stables, but the father was being led by his son. There would be a limit to the size of his wallet. But Ruben wasn't going to get into a bidding war. There was still room between the price he had offered to Helen and the amount which he might finally pay, but Ruben would exercise self control. He was not in a contest which he had to win. If he got the horse for reasonable money well and good. He was not going to get het up by a duel between himself and a man and boy. He did not have to win at any cost. Sometimes he was beaten. Sometimes people would not sell no matter what he offered. On this occasion Ruben knew that Helen was a seller. The approach by the man and boy was unexpected but it could be overcome.

He spoke directly to Martin.

"What do you want for this horse?" he asked.

Martin had an immediate answer.

"I want him to become a super horse," he said. "I want him to jump for gold. He can do it. I know that he can do it. All I want is for him to get his chance."

43

Ruben nodded understandingly.

"And do you think that you can give him that chance?" he asked.

Martin was silent. The dealer had got home with his question.

Donal Lynch spoke up.

"We'll give him a good life," he said. "He'll be well looked after. Martin knows about horses. He won't be neglected."

Ruben Bowden nodded his head.

"I know that you will give him the best," he said. "But will that be enough. Is that really what the boy wants"

He looked directly at the boy again.

Martin bit his lip. This man had a way of getting right to the heart of things.

"What will you do with him" he countered after a moment or two.

"I'll sell him on" the dealer said. "But he won't be going to a riding school. I'll sell him to professionals who will give him his chance as a showjumper. If he's as good as you think he is, he'll never look back. You'll see him on television at all the big shows. He might even become an international. Can you do that for him"

Defeated Martin silently shook his head. Donal Lynch felt for his son. It was a hard putdown but not cruelly meant. The dealer had spoken the truth. Martin could not give the horse his chance. He would have a good life at the Lynch home but he would be wasted. He would stand out in a field passing the years in idleness. With Ruben Bowden, Mustard would have the opening that could send him onwards to stardom.

Martin put out his hand to the dealer.

"Do your best for him" he said. "I'll being keeping a look out."

With that the boy turned his wheelchair around and moved away. Donal Lynch nodded to the others and followed his crippled son. He was pushing furiously at the wheels. Donal knew that inside, Martin was devastated. He had made the first big sacrifice of his life, but he had been realistic. A boy in a wheelchair could never ride a horse to win gold for Ireland. But he had made an important decision. Martin's ambition was not diminished by that decision. He had given Mustard his opportunity. The golden dun horse would go to people who would do what Martin could not. Mustard would have his chance at stardom and Martin would have the satisfaction of knowing that he had given him that chance.

Faith

Dan Loughlin was a healer. It was not a traditional calling passed down from father to son or even from distant relatives There was no history of such a profession in his family. He wasn't the seventh son of a seventh son. His practice of the art was founded purely on a need to have some kind of job. School for Dan Loughlin finished at fourteen years of age and without any further education but possessed of an innate cunning and ability to present himself well he had graduated into a profession which was revered and respected throughout the seven counties in which he had sought a living for nearly twenty years.

Dan had hit on his career by accident. An acknowledged and widely publicised faith healer had arrived in the little town in which Dan lived and in a moment of idle curiosity he had gone to see what it was all about. There was prayer, a laying on of hands and most importantly from Dan's standpoint the passing round of a collection box. Dan was twenty three at the time, had passed through several jobs, none of which generated any interest or lasting passion for him. In need of a career which would pay dividends, Dan convinced himself that he could do this job as well as anyone else.

The first few years were hit and miss. He made mistakes, but now after nearly two decades in the business, Dan had honed his act to plausible perfection and could lay on hands and lead his audience in meditation better than any other more genuine practitioner of the art, better than any priest, with a far superior veneer than the bedside manner of the best of doctors.

Dan had been smart enough to launch himself on his new career well away from his family and relations. He knew that he could not withstand the mockery of neighbours, the scepticism of people who knew him from childhood and would not in any circumstances consider him a person who had the credentials for the ministry of healing which he purported to practice.

Dan was under no illusions about himself. He knew that fundamentally he was a fraud, but he had nothing on his conscience. He instilled a feeling of well being amongst his clients, brought some comfort to those who were afflicted, and applied a panacea to people whose own imaginations convinced themselves that they were well. Dan Loughlin based his success on the fact despite the fact that he knew he had no power, some people were relieved of their pain mainly through their own confusion. Self suggestion was an important weapon in the Loughlin armoury. There would always be sufficient numbers of people who would claim that he had made them well to offset those who complained that he had brought them no benefit at all.

In the early years Dan toured from town to town, taking rooms in small hotels or setting up in local halls for nominal rents, depending on small advertisements in the local papers, posters, and after a year or two on word of mouth. People wanted to believe, some people were all the better for his ministrations, others showed no improvement, but the very fact that he was in business and available brought its own amount of free wheeling success.

When he had got enough money together Dan bought a small house, converted the lower floor into a reception area and a consulting room, and operated from this permanent base. There was easy parking and by dedicating himself to being in place for six full days a week, Dan made a good living. In the beginning he had grouped his clients together, giving a short homily, asking people to pray with him, and moving amongst the audience to lay hands on heads while apparently reciting a short prayer.

Since he had set himself up in his new surroundings, Dan had abandoned group sessions, saw everyone in private and individually and concentrated on creating a special rapport with those who sought relief from their troubles. Dan was astute enough never to claim that he could effect a cure. He offered counsel and support, there was no suggestion that he could achieve divine intervention, no claim that would bring him into conflict with either church or medicine.

The question of remuneration was also carefully handled. Dan charged no fixed fees. There was a box in the outer room into which people could put a donation. If asked how much, Dan responded that he would leave it to themselves. Whatever they could afford. Dan's life was dedicated to giving succour he implied, all he sought in return was a small gift with which to purchase life's necessities. The result was that people overpaid, anxious that they should not be found wanting in their contributions for services rendered.

The Corrigans brought their daughter on a cool but sunny day in early September. Sharon Corrigan was a tall thin girl with an air of lassitude that Dan immediately put down to a troubled mind. She was unnaturally pale had dark rings around her eyes and appeared to be totally disinterested in her surroundings or in the fact that she had been brought to a man who perhaps might have a solution to her problems.

Sharon didn't know that she had problems. She had shut out life and spent her days in lethargy and total disinterest in whatever was going on around her. Dan now had experience enough to put his finger on the source of Sharon's affliction. The problem was in her mind. She was the victim of severe depression and the place for her was surely in the care of a psychiatrist. Drugs and a regime of hospital care were the real answers to the problems of this stricken young woman.

The Corrigans were country folk. Dermot wrestled with a small farm which paid less and less over the years. His wife Sheila went out to work in a local supermarket to bring in the extra money that ensured that they survived in a self perpetuating round of debt and toil from which they could never hope to escape. Even in these days of national prosperity the Corrigans were marginalized, locked into a lifestyle that allowed no egress, no hope of escape. They were one family amongst the many thousands to whom national prosperity and profits had brought no relief.

Sharon was the one beacon of hope in their lives. She was their only child. When she was younger she was bright and vivacious, a willful, laughing, cheerful fountain of joy that brightened her parents grey existence. But as she grew older she changed. No longer was she the cheerful confiding daughter. The teenage years brought silence and temper, moods and sulkiness replaced the outgoing nature of her childhood years.

At first they thought that this was a passing phase and that as she grew older things would change. But Sharon grew more and more inward looking, more and more wan and pale, more and more uninterested in the active bubbling ingredients of a cheerful and happy life.

At first Dermot and Sheila did nothing. They waited in the vain hope that Sharon's spirit would return. Eventually they sought help but their GP was not accommodating. Like themselves he put Sharon's condition down to age and puberty, and advised them to ignore her tantrums. To respond to her onslaughts would only encourage her, Dr Thornton advised. Best to shoulder the immediate burden and let nature run its course.

They followed this advice for nearly a year gradually realizing that Sharon was getting worse not better. There were days when they could hardly get her out of bed, and when they did more often than not she took herself off for long walks alone. At least they presumed that they walked, although Dermot more than once had found her lying on the bales in the haybarn, apparently worn out by the small effort of having walked a few metres across the farm yard. Then there were the silences, long sullen silences with apparently no interest in talking to either of her parents or going out with friends, reading or even watching the television. The circles under Sharon's eyes grew darker, she lost weight and became a thin wasted parody of herself.

The Corrigans were under no illusions. Something was seriously wrong with their daughter and they could no longer postpone the search for help. Dr Thornton, finally convinced that things were not normal in Sharon's life, referred her to a psychiatrist. They had to pay for each consultation and the fees were yet another burden on their hard pressed financial situation. But neither Dermot nor Sheila begrudged the money. What was important was that Sharon should be well again. If necessary the farm could be sold to achieve that objective.

Dermot and Sheila decided that the psychiatric route was not for them when committal to a mental hospital was proposed as the only solution to Sharon's condition. Sharon needed long stay treatment. There was no other alternative, the psychiatrist assured them. He could do nothing for her. A strong regime of anti-depressant drugs was needed and it might be necessary for her to have electro convulsive therapy. Sharon's condition was deep rooted. The psychiatrist was kindly but uncompromising.

Dermot and Sheila were stricken. This was the last thing they wanted for Sharon. Acceptance of the fact that she might be mentally ill was one thing, but compliant acquiescence in confining their daughter to a mental hospital was a step too far. Once inside, she might ever come out. Then there was the stigma. What would the neighbours think, their friends. It would be impossible to conceal the fact that she had been committed. Indeed already there was talk. Sharon's situation had been difficult to keep hidden.

There was great sympathy for the family, but a general consensus that something had happened to Sharon, that she was not like other teenagers, that there was something wrong with her head. Had the Corrigans understood how fully aware their friends and neighbours were aware of Sharon's troubles, they might have been more agreeable to the solution proposed. But they were blissfully ignorant of the talk that had been going on around them for months. Everyone around knew that Sharon was sickly and strange and everyone was waiting for the family's next move.

It was Dermot Corrigan who had suggested an approach to Dan Loughlin. They had debated the awful prospect of Sharon's incarceration for nearly a week without coming up with any solution. To be placed in a mental hospital was worse than prison. At least if someone was sent to prison there was a reason. For their daughter to be confined indefinitely with other mental patients, controlled by drugs, regulated by doctors and nurses, to be able to make no choices of their own was something which her father could not accept. He knew what he would feel himself if he were forced to undergo such a regime. No matter how difficult was Sharon's problem there had to be a better way.

So they went to Dan Loughlin's house. It was a seventy kilometre round trip, but neither Sheila nor Sharon made any complaint. Sharon lounged indifferently in the back of the car, refusing to be drawn by her mother's attempts to make her notice some local landmark in passing. Neither did she pay any attention to her father's explanation of their journey. She wasn't interested in attempts to make her well, her sole concentration was on her own internal misery. Outside there was no other world, inside Sharon was content to languish in the torpor which her condition generated.

The healer studied the stricken young woman with some concern. He had dealt with cases of depression before, but this was a particularly difficult case. He was not even sure that depression was the issue, but for the moment he could put no other construction on it. He decided to talk to the girl in the absence of her parents and asked them to go to the outside room. Then settling back in his chair he started to probe. His first few questions were about familiar things, her family, her home, work on the farm. He elicited very little response. The girl seemed to be in a world of her own, making spasmodic replies, but clearly locked into her own particular empty universe.

Dan Loughlin ran over options in his mind. There had to be a reason, a root cause for this terrible loneliness in which the girl was sunk. He considered a list of possible influences, abuse perhaps, although the Corrigans seemed to be decent God fearing people. The healer was a good judge of character and circumstances. He had to be otherwise he would never succeed in breaking down the barriers that led to healing, particularly when the source of that healing lay within his clients themselves. He was certain that Dermot Corrigan had never abused his daughter. Such a thing was unthinkable, yet of course it happened amongst the most unlikely people. The couple, however, so clearly demonstrated honesty and integrity and acceptance of their responsibilities. No, abuse was not an issue here.

Bullying perhaps? The girl was seventeen, nearly eighteen perhaps, and she had put school behind her. There was no opportunity for anyone to badger her, apart of course from the parents, but again the healer passed them over. They were so clearly concerned about their daughter's well being, so obviously out of their depth that Loughlin knew that this too was not an issue.

52

FAITH

Had she doubts about her sexuality, he wondered. She was a tall and strikingly attractive young woman despite the pallor induced by her illness and the black circles underneath her eyes. Her hair had been washed that morning, not by the girl herself, Loughlin surmised, but by her mother, anxious to make her daughter as presentable as possible for this important outing. Could she have boyfriend trouble, he wondered, and probed gently for an answer. The girl gave no response. He wondered if she was attracted to her own sex and if self doubt lay behind her breakdown. It was a possibility, he thought and went on to search in a new direction.

Religion. Could that be an issue. She came from a devout, rural background that blindly accepted the guilt and oppression of the Catholic tradition. Loughlin himself had long ceased to be a believer. He had grown cynical in the face of the long procession of invalids and troubled people that came to his door. But he understood well enough that faith and a belief in God and a life after death, was an important, even a vital consolation for many people.

"Do you believe in God," he asked.

For the first time he struck a chord. She stirred slightly in her chair and for a brief moment focused her eyes on the healer.

"God has deserted me," she murmured indistinctly.

The healer leaned forward in his seat. He had got beyond the barrier. Certain that he was on a fruitful trail, he probed further.

"Why has God deserted you," he asked.

The girl looked him squarely in the face for the first time. Her eyes opened a little wider. For the first time there was some animation in her tone.

She was silent again.

"There's nothing there for me," she said. "I'm fed up with the farm. My parents work all the time It's no life."

"Why don't you go to work," the healer inquired.

"I'm ill," she said, subsiding again as the realization struck her that she needed to find support in her infirmity.

"Why are you ill," the healer asked.

There was another silence.

"God has struck out at me," she said eventually. "He is punishing me for my sins."

Dan Loughlin started to feel that he was getting somewhere. He had got this previously silent and withdrawn young woman to speak. That in itself was an achievement. Strengthened by this modest success he decided to follow the road that she had indicated. God and faith were obviously issues here. The girl had lost faith in the God that she had submitted to all her life.

54

FAITH

"Your sins can only be minor ones," he said soothingly.

He began to feel like a priest in the confessional.

"God will forgive you but he wants you to make an effort with your life," he went on.

The girl sat up in her seat and stared at him fixedly for a moment or two.

"I'm ill" she said finally, letting herself slouch again.

The healer nodded his agreement.

"You can cure yourself you know," he said. "You only need to make an effort. This thing in your head can be driven out. You will feel well again if you make the effort."

"God made me like this," she said.

The healer leaned forward and took up her hand.

"You weren't always this way," he said. "You parents told me. This is a new thing. Something happened to you. What was it?"

There was another silence.

"I had a baby," she said blankly. "I lost it. My parents didn't know."

She began to cry.

"God punished me for my sin," she said after a moment or two. "He destroyed my child."

She wiped her eyes with the back of her hand and stared

55

miserably at the healer.

"Did you tell anyone," he asked.

She shook her head.

"My parents would have been devastated," she said. "I went with a boy from the village. It was our first time. I didn't tell him or anyone else."

"It wasn't to be," the healer said.

He felt inadequate. How could he counsel this afflicted girl so oppressed with her misery.

"God has deserted me," she said again. "I'm alone. I don't know what to do."

"You have to get on with your life," he said eventually. "These things pass. You will get married someday and have other children."

The girl was not be mollified. She began to cry again. The healer got up and paced around the room. This was a new experience for him. Most of his cases had been with people troubled by their illnesses or by their family circumstances. His few words of consolation and the placing of his hands on their heads brought some relief to many, perhaps only a momentary easement, but it justified their visit and their contributions to the donations box. This was different, the usual ministration would not do. He was challenged by a very special ailment, by a fragile suffering mind. What he said and did could have substantial after effects.

He took the girl by the hand again and drew her out of the chair.

FAITH

"I want you to pray with me," he said softly, kneeling down at her feet. For a moment she stood over him but then she too sank to her knees. The healer desperately rummaged through his mind for old long forgotten prayers. Nothing suitable came to the surface. He would have to improvise.

"Lord," he intoned, "help us to overcome this time of pain and suffering. Forgive us the sin which has brought us such sorrow. Heal us and drive away this affliction which surrounds us. Give us a new life, and new hope for the future."

He looked at the girl. She had her eyes closed, drinking in the few hesitating words that he had strung together. The communicating door with the outside room swung open and Dermot Corrigan stood in the doorway. The healer motioned to him to go back outside. This was not a time for interruptions. After a few seconds hesitation the father closed the door again on his daughter and the healer.

Dan Loughlin lifted the girl up and settled her in her seat again. Some colour had found its way into her pallid cheeks. The healer seized the moment.

"You must have faith," he said. "The healing time has come. God will forgive you. You must believe in him."

The girl nodded and folded her hands together. The healer placed his hands on her head in his practiced manner and kept them there for a few moments. Then he brought the girl to her feet and took her by each hand.

"Do you understand," he asked urgently. "The bad times are over. You are renewed, refreshed. God has forgiven you. In return you must get well again."

The healer spoke from the heart. This troubled young woman had affected him. He had felt so helpless, yet somehow, by

57

some miracle he had got through to her. He was elated, for the first time in his long career he felt he had really accomplished something. It would be some yet before the girl was fully recovered but he had sent her out on a journey which would bring her peace and closure.

He went to the door and called her parents into the room.

"Sharon is feeling better now," he said an an uncharacteristically understated way. "You can take her home. She will recover fully in time. I guarantee it."

And he could give such a guarantee. He had healed a suffering soul. The era of cynical espousal of his well rehearsed routine with its ill deserved monetary contributions was over. Dan Loughlin had become a true healer. For the first time in twenty years he had real faith in his ability not just to bring comfort and solace to the afflicted, but to truly work miracles on their behalf. Dan Loughlin now fully deserved the title which he had given himself many years ago. He was Dan Loughlin the healer. It was a claim which he could justifiably and in good conscience make to those who came to seek his help in future

Truth

"We can't print this!"

Matt Dillon looked his news editor straight in the eye. Joe McEvoy could be faced down by reporters who were tough enough to do so. Dillon had every confidence in his story. He had worked on it for weeks, interviewed a string of sources and made various attempts to doorstep the subject of his two thousand word long piece. It was an expose. Worth a lead in on page one and the half page inside which it would fill.

McEvoy, however was not as susceptible as usual. In fact he was downright obdurate.

"Its dangerous, libelous, short on verifiable facts and you haven't got any quotes from the man himself. He has a right to give his side of the story."

"He wouldn't co-operate," Matt protested. "I went to his house on four or five occasions. He refused to talk to me."

"That's no excuse," the news editor responded flatly. "You're obliged to give his side of the story. Without it there's nothing printable."

"It's hard fact," Dillon protested. "I checked every line. Jack O'Neill is bent. He's been taking bribes and everyone knows it. The other papers will get this as sure as anything. We've got to run with it now, while we have an exclusive."

The news editor slapped Matt's pages of typescript down on his desk.

"It's too risky," he said in a quieter tone. "He'll sue for sure. He would have to. His whole credibility would be destroyed if he ignored the story. Not that he's going to get any opportunity to either accept it or deny it," McEvoy went on in a louder more forceful tone. "We're not running it and that's final."

He pushed the sheets of copy back at Matt and leaned back in his chair, a look of finality and decisiveness on his face.

Matt, however, was not giving up.

"If I get a quote from him will you run it," he asked.

The other thought for a few moments.

"If he admits that he took bribes for re-zoning, we'll run it," he said grudgingly. "Not that you're likely to get such an admission. And it will have to be on tape," he warned to Matt's retreating back. "We have to have proof. Proof that will stand up in court."

Matt went back to his desk, satisfied that he had won a marginal victory. The news editor had qualified his rejection of the piece by demanding proof and an admission by Jack O'Neill.

He was under no illusions about the difficulties that lay ahead. He had worked hard on his story for several weeks, filing his assigned daily markings for the newsroom and making his enquiries into Jack O'Neill's corruption at night. There was no shortage of people prepared to claim that O'Neill was corrupt, but no one as yet had been prepared to come forward with the proof that the news editor had so adamantly demanded. Matt's sources were anonymous. The lack of a named informant struck down the story's credibility.

Proof, that was the sticking point. There were two roads to travel. The first was to get someone to admit that they had paid O'Neill a bribe. The second was to get O'Neill to admit that he had taken one. There had to be a reason for money changing hands of course. Matt was certain that he was not short of options here. Jack O'Neill had been the prime mover of several controversial rezonings and breach of the county development plan. Where he led other councillors in his party would follow. It might even be the case that O'Neill passed on a share of the spoils.

Matt wasn't too concerned about the other councillors. Jack O'Neill was his prime target. It was personal. O'Neill had blocked him from getting perfectly legitimate stories on council affairs. He was an old fashioned mogul, one who believed that as little as possible should be said to reporters. His business on behalf of the council was private and he gave no interviews or statements to the press.

Jack O'Neill had held office as a county councillor for over twenty years. He knew what it was all about. Votes counted, not newspaper stories. Jack O'Neill knew how to garner votes. By his lights he was a good councillor. He looked after his people. Matt gave him full credit for this, but a story was a story and he knew in his heart that O'Neill was dirty, that planning permissions and zonings were bought and paid for and that in the long run the public lost out. Shopping centres were built in unsuitable locations, housing estates went up without proper services and facilities, roads were unnecessarily cut through green belt agricultural land.

Matt had one solid lead. A disgruntled constituent who had sought and received planning permission for some but not all of his land despite paying out to Jack O'Neill had been an off the record source. If Matt could get him to go public with his information, he was on a winner. O'Neill would be forced into making some sort of comment, probably a denial, but if the witness was revealing enough, the story would stand up. Matt decided to make a further effort to get his man to talk.

Art O'Callaghan was a farmer who eked out a living on seventy acres of grass. He ran a beef herd and like most farmers in this field suffered from the fact that costs were rising, prices were coming down and there seemed little long term hope of survival. The prospect of selling his land to developers was enticing. The catch of course was the zoning. His land was designated agricultural and until the question of a sale to builders came up, Art had no thought at all of selling off what had been a farm inherited down the line from his grandfather. Now there was nothing in farming only debt and hardship. The first cautious approach from a Dublin developer had given the farmer new hope. His farm was about three miles from the town, but was good flat land and approached by a secondary road. The agent who had come down from Dublin explained what was involved. They were taking options on land which in due course might be used for housing.

"We have to think years ahead," the agent had explained. "We believe that the town will expand in this direction. It is only a matter of time, but there will have to be changes in the development plan if things are going to work out.

Art O'Callaghan wasn't really interested in options. They offered a short term solution to his cash flow problems right enough, but at the end of the day he wanted to sell the farm for its true development value. A sale for housing would give him a substantial lump of cash on which to base his future.

"If I had planning permission," he said to the agent cautiously. "What would be the position."

"We'd take a fresh look at things," was the response. "You'd get the commercial rate for an approved site. But this is down to you. We can't do anything at local level. You'll have to work it out for yourself."

He could have added that his firm had been stung on too many previous occasions. Getting land rezoned was a treacherous procedure and expensive too. Now the firm's policy was to let the landowner get planning permission and negotiate the best possible deal for themselves after that.

Matt left the office and drove out to Art O'Callaghan's farm. The road just outside the town was lined with travellers caravans and carts. Rubbish of all kinds festooned the roadside ditches, old clothes, mattresses, tyres and motor car parts. One or two horses grazed the roadside grass, unconcerned at passing traffic, and a bevy of mixed breed dogs and small dirty children played amidst the trash. Social housing for travellers was one of the county council's stated aims but a supply of houses had been a long time coming. The Council was mandated by legislation to provide housing and services halting sites, but the years went by and successive traveller generations were still living on the side of the road.

Art O'Callaghan was in his home, muddy boots thrown off and relaxing after a day's toil on the land. It wasn't easy looking after a suckler herd, calves got sick, there was the ever increasing cost of feed, and the enormous amount of paper work demanded by the Department of Agriculture, but there were farmers who had a much harder life. The twice daily grind of milking for instance. There was the security of the monthly milk cheque but margins were as tight in milk as they were in beef.

O'Callaghan had embarked on his decision to sell the farm with some reluctance but with an ever increasing realization that there was no other course. He either had to sell up or expand and expansion wasn't an option. It was time to get out. Rezoning, with a subsequent lucrative sale to the developers from Dublin, was the way forward. But to embark on that route entailed a substantial bribe to Jack O'Neill. Twenty thousand was the sum demanded and raising it had exhausted all O'Callaghan's ready money plus a substantial increase in his overdraft, but the prospect of getting a big price for his land had justified the outlay. He would be debt for a time, but the big cheque that was in the offing would clear all that was owed.

O'Callaghan paid over the money and waited for the council meeting that would fulfill his ambitions. The rezoning went through all right. Jack O'Neill was as good as his word, but there was an unforeseen and unfortunate codicil to the decision. All seventy acres bar a small parcel around Art's yard and dwelling house were zoned residential. That was what Art had paid for. But the subsection of the permission brought an angry and aggressive constituent to Jack O'Neill's door. Ten acres of Art's land was set aside for social housing for travellers. The new housing estate from which Art would derive his future capital and profits would march side by side with the dirt and filth of a travellers settlement.

Jack O'Neill was unrepentant. Travellers had to be accommodated as well as settled people, he told O'Callaghan. It was the law. There were harsh words and strong language. O'Callaghan wanted his money back. The councillor brushed him off. O'Callaghan had wanted his land re-zoned. O'Neill had done his bit.

Art went home an extremely dissatisfied customer. He didn't even have to contact the development company to know that they would now be uninterested in his lands. The company specialized in up market housing at premium prices. Their margins would not be sustainable. Professional people wouldn't want to live side by side with travellers. Art had paid out his bribe of twenty thousand for nothing.

The builders were quick to scuttle their verbal deal with the farmer. The zoning conditions had been published in the local paper and their agent had sent a cutting off to headquarters.

TRUTH

There was now no prospect of them buying Art's land, even at a reduced price. A firm of their standing did not engage with itinerants. Their customers wanted their housing estates to be pristine and well located. Neighbours of such low social standing and filthy habits could not be countenanced.

This was the state of play when Matt Dillon came knocking on Art O'Callaghan's door once more. He knew the pressure the farmer was under. O'Callaghan was a bubble ready to burst. He had refused to name O'Neill on Matt's last visit but he had confirmed that cash had been handed over. What Matt needed now was a full statement, an outright naming of the councillor.

An angry O'Callaghan was almost at breaking point. He was thirsting for revenge but didn't know how to get it. Bribing a county councillor was a serious offence. If the farmer publicly revealed his role in the affair both he and O'Neill could be prosecuted. He could go to jail. Matt Dillon counselled otherwise. The authorities would be more interested in nailing the councillor than going after the whistle blower. There were other guilty men, other surreptitious transactions. Outing O'Neill would open the whole sorry business to scrutiny. O'Callaghan's part would be overlooked in the onslaught which would be directed at the guilty councillors. Art O'Callaghan was doing a public service by exposing the rot of local politics.

Matt Dillon kept pressurizing the farmer. He wanted O'Callaghan to spell out exactly what had transpired between himself and Jack O'Neill. At first O'Callaghan was cautious, an innate cunning warning him that he should say as little as possible.

"You can bring O'Neill down," the reporter said encouragingly. "Let the public know exactly what he has been up to. If you do the thing right you'll get your own back and put an end to this sort of blackmail as well."

65

The farmer considered this for a moment or two.

"I don't want to get myself into trouble," he said. "I'll have to admit that I paid over the money. People will think I'm a mug."

"They'll see that you're not man who can be made a fool of" Matt replied. "Jack O'Neill will have to take the consequences."

The farmer hesitated again. Matt said nothing. He didn't want to overplay his hand. Finally O'Callaghan made up his mind.

"Alright I'll give it all to you. You can print it and damn the consequences."

He recounted the story of his trouble with the farm, his approach to the Dublin developer, and his decision to get the land rezoned. O'Neill had taken the bribe and the planning process took its course.

"The whole deal has been destroyed," the farmer burst out angrily. "I won't get the money for the land now. No one will want to build expensive houses beside a travellers' camp. Jack O'Neill has ruined me. I borrowed money from the bank to pay him and I have no chance of paying it back."

Matt went in hard to doubly confirm the farmer's statement. He wanted to get a clear admission on the tape. His news editor would have no excuse to spike the story.

"You're telling me quite categorically that you bribed Jack O'Neill to get you planning permission," he said underscoring his previous questions and Art O'Callaghan's admissions.

"I did," the farmer reaffirmed. "I paid the bastard up front. You can print that. Every word of it is the truth."

TRUTH

Matt left O'Callaghan's house on a high. He had got himself a scoop. He would have to put the thing to Jack O'Neill, of course, but it didn't matter whether he confirmed or denied the farmer's story. Art O'Callaghan had implicated the councillor. O'Neill was finished. Next week's paper would bring him down.

Acting on a sudden impulse, Matt stopped his car at the row of roadside caravans on the way back into the town. He knocked on the door of one of the caravans and a young woman came out. Matt was surprised. She was good looking, well dressed and as far as he could see appeared to be clean. Her hair had recently been washed. For a moment Matt was at a loss. Evidently the travellers' world had changed. The girl was as stylish as any of those that could be seen around the town.

He introduced himself and told her that he was writing an article about the new homes that were planned for travellers.

The girl grinned.

"They've been telling us that for years," she said cynically. "I'll believe it when I see it."

"The Council have zoned the land," he said. "They're taking over ten acres to build houses. It won't take that long to do it. You should be moved in within a year."

The girl laughed.

"The Council's word means nothing," she said. "The councillors are a pack of liars. We've been promised homes for the past ten years. Nothing has happened. We don't even have a halting site. How would you like to live on the side of the road," she demanded in a sudden flash of temper.

A few other people appeared from the caravans further down

the road.

"That's right" a man in a tee shirt said. "They're all liars, the whole bloody lot of them. They don't care about us. Those houses will never be built. People will object to them and we'll still be living here in ten years time."

Matt was disconcerted. He had thought he was bringing good news. But apparently no one was interested. There had been too many unkept promises in the past. These people just didn't believe it.

He got back in the car and drove to Jack O'Neill's smart house on the far side of the town. His reception by the travellers had deflated him slightly. His elation at getting the story from O'Callaghan was tempered by the sheer disbelief of the roadside people. The Council had been tried in the past and had been found wanting. The roadside people had been disappointed too many times.

Jack O'Neill heard him out in silence.

"I deny everything," he said flatly. "If you print anything about this I'll sue."

"Art O'Callaghan has gone on the record," Matt rejoined. "We're going to run the story. Now is the chance to have your say."

"I deny it," the councillor responded again, this time with a raised voice and a faint flush in his face. "It's all lies. You can't prove anything."

Matt left. He had fulfilled his duty. O'Neill had been given an opportunity to put his side of the case and had denied it. Matt would print that denial. He had got his quotes from both sides. The story had balance. There was no onus on the reporter to take any further action.

Matt's story was the front page lead when the paper came out. There was a rush on the newsagents as word got around and it was clear that they could have sold more copies if they had the foresight to do an extra run. People stopped Matt in the street to congratulate him. He was the local hero. Everyone was enthralled by his skilful exposure of local villains. Matt walked on air for a few days. He had made his mark with a sensational piece of writing that had caught the imagination of the public.

There were strong words about Jack O'Neill and the councillor came under serious pressure. Art O'Callaghan suffered less odium but no one praised him for coming forward. He was as corrupt as Jack O'Neill. Privately many people thought that he should have kept his mouth shut. He had dug his own grave, he deserved his fate, people decided, and he would have to live with the consequences.

An emergency meeting of the Council was called for later in the week. Jack O'Neill resigned a few hours before it was due to take place. There was only one item on the agenda. The councillors took less than half an hour to deal with it. The zoning of Art O'Callaghan's farm was revoked. His holding remained agricultural land, its value diminished, its owner virtually penniless. There would be no rich developer coming down from Dublin with a cheque.

Matt left the meeting and walked down the steps to the street. No houses would be built of Art O'Callaghan's land. The councillors had moved to protect themselves. They would have nothing to do with Jack O'Neill's dealings. By scrapping the zoning altogether they had distanced themselves from Jack O'Neill's handiwork. Matt was thoughtful, worried even. Matt had done his work well. There was nothing wrong with his story. He had told the truth giving an even hand to both sides. The Council had firmly declared that it wanted nothing more to do with Art O'Callaghan's land. The original process was tainted. The councilors wanted to protect themselves. The zoning had to be thrown out to ensure that no other councillor would be tarnished. But still something niggled at Matt's conscience. Things had not quite as they should be. There had been unexpected spin off. The Council's decision had implications for more people than Art O'Callaghan.

The girl from the campsite had been in the public seats and followed him out catching him by the arm.

"You see," she said.   I told you so. There'll never be houses built for travellers. I spoke the truth. You can't deny it."

Pride

A decision had to be made. Stanley and Michelle argued about it constantly for nearly a week. It was all down to Michelle's preoccupation with their social status. The argument was whether their nine years old daughter, Naomi, should go to ballet classes or Irish dancing. Naomi herself had expressed an interest in going to the weekly Irish dancing class in the local hall. Michelle wanted her to go to the ballet lessons staged every Wednesday afternoon in the function room of the Gondolier Hotel.

Michelle had her priorities. She was conscious of her social standing. They, the Nolans, lived in one of the better class housing estates on the outskirts of the town, drove two cars, and generally spent most of Stanley's salary on living up to the standards which Michelle had set for them. Stanley was an executive with a Dublin electronics company and visited plants around the country which meant that he was often away from home. Michelle compensated for his absence by spending the bulk of his relatively modest salary on extra furnishings and fripperies for the house, new clothes for herself and Naomi, and a range of fancy foods and French wines which she maintained were an essential part of living the life which their place in small town society demanded.

There was nothing unusual about Michelle's appetite for the finer things of life. The neighbouring wives also traded their husband's salaries for a range of exotic foods and fancy clothes and furnishings. Some of the wives went out to work themselves, but Michelle had eschewed such a practice. For one thing, she wasn't really qualified to take up a job which would adequately compensate for the time demanded. There was the extra cost of child care for Naomi to think of if she went out to work.

They spent quite a lot of money on baby sitters as it was. When Stanley was at home at week-ends or the occasional weeknight when he was not away on his company's business,

Michelle dragged him out to every local happening. She had a preference for anything which had a cultural flavour but no occasion was too small or unassuming to allow Michelle to show off her latest dress, her special hairdo, her carefully cultivated smart accent. The Rotary Club, the Chamber of Commerce, the Heritage Society, the golf club, all offered outlets for Michelle's constant pursuit of status and style.

Stanley was a patient man, but there were times when Michelle's drive to become the first lady of the town became too much to handle. He wanted to relax when he came home, his work entailed long journeys across the country, and he was often tired and in no form for a round of social engagements. But Michelle was indefatigable. She went everywhere, with or without or husband, and reveled in the belief that she was important and in demand.

She was constantly pressing Stanley for money to maintain her pretentious lifestyle.

"I need a new dress" she would say to him in a tone that brooked no resistance, seizing his credit card to ensure that her onslaught on the shops would not be limited to a dress alone. Other accessories might be needed, a handbag perhaps, or a new pair of shoes.

Stanley put up with his wife's extravagance, ignored her occasional complaints that he should look for a rise or get a better paying job. He was happy in his employment, was satisfied with his house and his company car, and was absorbed with his daughter's growing list of childhood accomplishments. He had no objection to dancing classes of any kind but the issue of ballet and Irish dancing was yet another of Michelle's examples of self indulgence. Michelle was a snob and things with a particular perspective Naomi herself wanted to join the Irish dancing classes. Stanley felt that for once her wishes should be granted and that social pretension should take second place.

"Let Naomi make up her own mind," he urged. "She knows what she wants to do. She should be allowed to chose for herself. You're too much of a control freak."

"I know what's best," Michelle responded sharply, resenting his description of her. "Ballet is the place for her. She'll enjoy and meet nice children."

Meeting nice children was the underlying thrust of Michelle's decision. Nice children meant nice parents and nice she translated as families which were affluent, whose husband's held down good jobs and were socially acceptable.

Michelle was adamant and her partner as usual bowed before her onslaught. Michelle had her own evaluation of the comparative merits of ballet and Irish dancing. The kids from the council estates went to Irish dancing, it was a lower class pursuit. Ballet offered a new cultural dimension to their own and their daughter's lives. Naomi's attendance was another weapon in Michelle's formidable armoury of social elan. It would be a good conversational gambit to be able to talk about Naomi and her ballet classes. Irish dancing certainly didn't have the same cachet.

The battle with Stanley was relatively short and bloodless. Stanley gave in. Michelle as usual got her way. A little pink leotard was purchased for Naomi along with soft ballet shoes and Michelle added another car journey to her already packed driving schedule. She drove Naomi backwards and forward to the ballet classes without complaint. There were many demands on her time but nothing was too exhausting or time consuming for Michelle in her determination to ensure that the Nolan family were a step up from the rest of the community.

Stanley often wondered where it would all end. He was permanently in debt and the annual holidays at various Continental resorts and Michelle's quest for week-end breaks in the more acceptable Irish resorts, or shopping trips to Dublin's Grafton street, were a constant depletion of his earnings. The bank overdraft and credit card repayments ensured that he had no savings to speak of. Life for Stanley Nolan was a constant pursuit of cash to maintain a style of living which he could not really afford. He managed to manipulate his traveling expences occasionally to provide some small amounts of extra cash, but the firm's accountants were eagle eyed and he had to be cautious. Stanley loved his wife and child but he often wondered whether he made the right decision when he embarked on life's voyage with Michelle.

"We're spending too much money," he would grumble occasionally when his credit card limit was reached or a timely reminder about the state of his overdraft came from the bank manager. "We must cut down. We'll get into trouble if we don't"

His words fell on deaf ears. Michelle was not responsive. Her shopping sprees continued unabated and there was constant pressure, not just about finances but about engaging in the many activities at which Michelle felt they should be seen. Stanley counted himself lucky that he had a good secure job which gave him regular breaks from the marital home. He was able to escape from many of Michelle's social forays and on other occasions resignedly acquiescing in a lifestyle to which he did not really wish to engage and could not afford. It had to come to an end, of course, his salary could not support the spiralling cost of Michelle's grand view of affairs, but when the axe fell it came with an unexpected brutality.

Stanley's firm went bust. The staff were laid off with their only entitlement the statutory redundancy payments and suddenly Stanley was reduced to drawing the dole. He accepted the cards which fate had dealt with his customary equanimity, confident that in the country's current era of remarkable prosperity that he would soon get another job. Michelle, however, was stricken. Stanley came home unexpectedly and broke the terrible news. Michelle was faced with the need to trim her sails, cut back on delicatessen luxuries, do without shopping trips to Dublin and week-ends away. One of the cars would have to be sold, and there was a question of whether or not they could afford the payments on the mortgage.

Michelle was devastated, Stanley phlegmatic and unexpectedly tough. Things were going to be difficult he told his wife, and she could cut out her nonsense and get down to the adoption of a more frugal lifestyle. She had the additional burden of coping with a husband who was at home during the day, never went away on business, and who became more and more morose as the months drew on as it became clear that getting a new job was going to be a much more difficult proposition than he had anticipated.

Stanley was fortynine. His whole career had been with the same firm, and there were apparently few openings for middle aged executives in the electronics field. The sector had been suffering cutbacks. There were problems internationally and there was a surplus of people with his particular expertise. He applied for other jobs, but without success. Stanley it seemed had few qualifications for alternative employment and his age was also a factor. Industry wanted bright young men, with the emphasis it seemed on young.

Michelle displayed unexpected fortitude in adversity. She raised no objection when her car was sold and the money allocated to a suddenly pressing bank. The Nolans learned for themselves one of the fundamentals of banking. There was no room for sentiment when it came to dealing with customers who were in trouble. The bank wanted its money and was not prepared to do any deals. The family, the bank manager told Stanley would have to live within its means from now on. Stanley glumly agreed and settled down to educating his wife about the economics of life on the dole.

Secretly Stanley was slightly relieved at the curtailing of his wife's extravagance. He regretted losing his job, but when cutbacks in the home were implemented, he wasn't really that much worse off. His personal circumstances were relatively unchanged. He had never had much money in his pocket so the new privation which affected his wife made little difference to himself.

Michelle said nothing to the neighbours. He was sure that they had noticed the fact that the car was gone but no one made any comment. It could be assumed, she consoled herself, that they were contemplating a newer model. She was ready to make this excuse if the issue was raised, but nothing was said and she was spared the necessity of an outright lie. The fact that Stanley had stopped going off to work every day was another matter which bothered her at first, but again nothing was said and Michelle convinced herself that no one was any the wiser about their change of circumstances.

Life went on and gradually they became used to their new lifestyle. Michelle missed the trips to the shops in Dublin but managed to keep up appearances by responding to any invitation that came her way. She discovered that it was possible to enjoy a small town social life on a small budget. A new dress was not required for every social occasion. She still went to parties and decided to ignore the fact that they could not afford to reciprocate with any function of their own.

Things were not so difficult after all. Occasionally she regretted that she had been so extravagant in the past. Money put by instead would have been useful now, but behind her frivolity, Michelle was a sharp and understanding woman. She decided not to look back and concentrated on making the best of those opportunities that came her way.

She suffered a further traumatic blow when Stanley announced that they couldn't afford to keep up with Naomi's ballet classes. This was a step too far for Michelle. She had gone along with all the other privations, but now her daughter's status was threatened as well as her own. People would notice that Naomi had been taken out of class. This more than anything else would be a major breach in Michelle's attempts to hide the truth. If they could not afford to pay the fees for Naomi's ballet they must be in serious trouble. This surely was the blow which would totally diminish their standing in the neighbourhood.

"We can't do this," she told her husband only a step away from tears. "Naomi loves her ballet. She would be devastated if we took her out."

"Naomi can go to Irish dancing," Stanley replied cuttingly. "The lessons are cheaper. She will enjoy it just as much. That's what she wanted in the first place. It's only your ego that sent her to ballet. Now we can't afford the cost. You'll just have to accept how things are. I'm unemployed, on the dole, and the money isn't there any more."

Michelle cried at this riposte but Stanley was adamant. Her tears soon turned to rage. Her compliant husband of twenty years of marriage had turned into an ogre. He was short and cutting with her and refused point blank to sanction any expenditure over the weekly budget which they set themselves for household necessities. But to stop Naomi's ballet classes. It was a terrible blow to Michelle's self esteem. Consideration for her daughter didn't really come into it. Michelle was hurting but she was hurting for herself.

Stanley got his way. Naomi was taken out of ballet and for a week or two had an empty afternoon to fill. Finally Stanley went along to the hall to see if he could enroll Naomi in the dancing class. The decision brought a happy smile to the child's face. This was what she really wanted. Her mother's social dimension to her schedule of carefully selected activities was well over Naomi's head. She wanted to have fun, and ballet had been stern and uncompromising. The steps were difficult, the teacher sternly committed to securing perfection. Naomi was a carefree bubbling child and had longed to be to get away from Miss Carroll's discipline. The move to Irish dancing was greeted enthusiastically.

Michelle stayed away. She left it to Stanley to drive Naomi to her class every week and deliberately held herself aloof from the child's happy chattering account of each clearly enjoyable session. Stanley scraped up the few pounds necessary to get Noami her buckled black dancing shoes. The costume would come later. Most of the other children at the class danced in their everyday clothes. Costumes were for competitions which were as yet down the line. Michelle kept her distance. Normally she would have been the one at the shops attending to her daughter's needs but she was determined that she would make her disapproval clear to Stanley. Her husband had demeaned her by taking their daughter to such a common pursuit.

Naomi was a success. She quickly mastered the steps and made new friends. Michelle was torn in two directions. Her daughter was so obviously happy and enamoured with her dancing. But Michelle could not forgive the terrible blow to her self esteem that her husband had administered. Despite the tugs at her heartstrings caused by her daughter's obvious happiness she would not give in. Stanley made his first friendships with the other parents. The dancing class created its own bonds, for the parents as well as the children. For some Irish dancing was a pleasant pastime, not to be taken too seriously. For others there was the drive to be on top, to carry off medals and trophies. Michelle had her counterparts in every walk of life.

Stanley too was keen for his daughter to succeed, although not for the same reasons as had motivated his wife when she sent their daughter to the ballet classes.

"You've got to work at it," Stanley told his daughter. "You've got to be better than the other girls if you want to win competitions"

Naomi worked at it, not because she wanted to laud it over anyone but because she enjoyed the classes. They were cheerful. The music was lively, the beat of the children's dancing feet reverberated through the hall, and there was teasing and laughter when someone found themselves out of step and came crashing to a halt.

Stanley made friends with two of the mothers. This was not surprising. Fathers were normally at work and it was the women who brought their children to the classes. They were pleasant unassuming women and Stanley enjoyed their company. He would never be unfaithful to his wife no matter how much she provoked him, but it was nice to have alternative friendships based on a common interest.

Valerie and Marie Clare both lived in council houses, but they were smart and well spoken. Valerie's husband worked for the electricity company and Marie Clare's was a truck driver. Both families had an income away above that currently enjoyed by Michelle and Stanley. He wasn't concerned. He was learning to live with in straightened circumstances. But he welcomed the friendship, limited though it was. It was less of a strain to mix with these working class mothers than with Michelle's high rolling associates and Stanley warmed to them accordingly.

It was Valerie who first suggested that Naomi should compete at a dancing contest. She had closely followed Naomi's progress as well as that of her own daughter. Michelle mentioned it to the dancing teacher who reacted positively. Naomi was rapidly becoming one of her better pupils and she had reached the stage where she could go out and hold her own against any child of the same age.

Marie Clare warned Stanley that things were tough out there. Her daughter was older than Valerie's Angela, and had danced in several competitions. She had a green and red costume with a row of medals stitched to it and was clearly one of the better ambassadors for the dancing class.

Stanley listened to the voice of experience and was characteristically cautious. He didn't want to push Naomi on too soon. There was also the question of the costume. This would have to be bought and paid for. Valerie had an answer to this dilemma. She suggested it diffidently, not wanting to speak out of turn but shrewdly suspecting that there was some sort of family dispute behind Naomi's attendance at the dancing class.

"Some of the girls have grown out of their costumes," she said carefully. "You could buy one second hand. Some of the mothers would be glad to hand them on."

Stanley considered the suggestion. Stanley was a little concerned that his daughter would be wearing second hand clothes but pragmatically he decided that what Valerie said made sense. Inquiries amongst the other mothers produced a number of offers. The costumes were brought to the next class and Stanley carefully went through them, looking for the least worn as well as the one which was the best bargain.

He brought the costume home one evening. Michelle hit the roof berating her husband for once again bringing them downwards in the social scale. Stanley ignored her. There was a time when he would have submitted utterly in the face of his wife's onslaught but that day was gone. Stanley, stripped of his job and on the dole, was a better man than he had been in times of comparative affluence. He cut his wife off abruptly, and urged Naomi to get into the costume. It fitted well and Naomi was transported. All that remained was for her to get up on the stage and dance her way to a medal.

The day of the first competition came. Naomi was up well before breakfast time and resplendent in her new costume rushed into her parent's bedroom and wrestled them awake. Stanley got up immediately. He too was exuberant and cheerful. This was Naomi's big day. He washed and shaved and went downstairs to try and settle his daughter down. There were several hours to go before they needed to go down to the hall. Michelle stayed in bed, sulky, part of her offended that she was being left out of the day's celebrations, another part stiffly embittered about the fact that her husband had so callously ignored her wishes and enrolled their daughter in a pastime which was so clearly beneath them

Stanley brought his daughter to the hall, mingled with other excited parents and children and waited patiently while each of the contestants took their turn on the platform. The music was lively, provided by a pianist and a fiddler, and each child danced their hearts out. Stanley sat tensely in his seat when it came to Naomi's turn. To his eyes her performance was faultless. His golden haired daughter was a vision on the stage, dancing so blithely and confidently. The atmosphere was electric. There were hundreds of children there of course. Entries had come from Irish dancing schools all over the province and every child gave their utmost. Three judges sat at a table in front of the stage and frowningly marked down their scores.

It was well into the evening when the prize giving

commenced. Stanley and Naomi sat on the edges of their seats waiting impatiently for Naomi's section to be called. She had danced against children of her own age and the prizes would be awarded for the best of that category. Finally it was her age group's turn to hear their result. There was an expectant hush in the hall as everyone waited for the senior judge to deliver the verdict. Naomi bit her lip and waited. The pressure was unbearable for Stanley. A great cheer went up from Naomi's classmates when her name was called. She turned and kissed her father on the cheek and ran up to the stage to receive her medal and trophy. Stanley clapped and cheered frantically. Naomi had won through. His daughter was a winner. Exultantly he responded to the congratulations from the people around him and shook hands with as many as he could.

At the back of the hall Michelle stood alone, a tear trickling slowly down her face. She hadn't been able to stay away despite her dispute with Stanley and her distaste for the choice which had been forced upon them. It was so different from what she had wanted for her daughter. But it was Naomi's day and she was her mother. She had a mother's pride in her daughter's achievement. A medal for Naomi after all had its own kind of distinction.

Laughter

"There's no easy way to say this. I have to let you go."

The two old friends faced each other in the circus boss's caravan, cups of tea and biscuits spread out on the table in front of them. The clown looked his companion in the eye.

"I've worked with Carey's Circus for thirty six years," he said incredulously. "You can't do this. Where would I go. What would I do."

Chris Carey shifted uncomfortably in his seat. He hated doing this, but the financial pressures on his family's one hundred and twenty year's old business were intense. Billy Duffy wasn't the only who would be getting the bullet. At least fifteen other men would have to go, musicians, trapeze artists, animal trainers, roustabouts. These people Carey could dismiss without a great deal of thought. They were casual workers, tied to the circus by no more than a verbal contract for the season. After that they moved on. It was the way things were. Most people accepted the situation and organized their lives accordingly.

With a clown, however, it was different. The circus didn't sack its clowns. The laughing cheerful men in outlandish clothes and huge shoes with their white faces and thick red lips and bulbous noses, were such an integral part of circus life that they seemed to go on for ever. Their duties, of course, were not confined to the ring. They doubled up as box office attendants, casual labourers, sweepers, and extras in other acts. The clown has many faces, the painted masks imposed upon their features indelibly stamped on the minds of the audience, adults and children alike, for all their lives

Billy Duffy had been a clown for over fifty years. He came from a family of clowns, the trade handed down over the generations, their workplaces circuses all over Europe. The act never varied, a rolling rollicking whirlwind of fun, gymnastics, foolish escapades, and rough and tumble.

Now this was coming to an end. Billy Duffy had never married and there was no one to come after him. The heritage would be lost when he retired. To Billy that day had always seemed a long way off. Now, however, it had become immediate and urgent, casting a threatening shadow over his life and prospects. He looked appealingly at Carey, but the circus owner was immersed in his own thoughts, his own woes, and was totally unaware of his old friends tremulous scrutiny.

Outside the Big Top was coming down. The circus was moving on to another pitch in another town. An elephant trumpeted, one of the prancing Arab horses whinnied, there was the crash of toppling poles and some hearty swearing by the roustabouts. The sounds and smells of the circus were in Billy Duffy's blood. To leave all this behind was unthinkable, the parting would be almost like death itself, final absolute, no coming back.

Chris Carey came out of his reverie and getting up went to a drawer bringing out an envelope. He handed it to Billy.

"This is your wages and a bit more besides. It's all I can do. I'm sorry. If there was any other way…"

He broke off conscious again of the clown's misery and bemusement.

"You'll get another job," he said sympathetically. "There's always room for a good clown."

Billy shook his head.

"If that was true there'd be room for me here," he said resignedly. "I wouldn't be getting the sack."

He took the envelope and put into his pocket, but made no move to leave.

Tell me the truth," he said to Carey. "Why me. Why not one of the others. Your father and I soldiered together with this circus. He was my best friend. I thought you and I were friends as well."

Carey avoided his glance. He didn't want to tell Billy that falling attendances and serious cash flow problems were only part of the truth, that he had picked out Billy because he was too old for the job, no longer agile, slow to get up after his tumbles, his voice no longer carrying to the audience, losing that vital credibility as a cheerful perpetrator of side splitting mishaps that brought the laughs.

But in his heart Billy knew the score. He was a stiff old man who had gone well beyond his prime. He couldn't do handstands any more, found it hard to run, jump and cavort with his fellow clowns. He was breathless after every stint in the ring, and stumbled through routines that at one time had scarcely challenged his physical prowess. Time had caught up on Billy Duffy. He had heard the last call of the ringmaster and it was not a pleasant experience.

Wearily he got up, his tiredness evident in his bowed frame, and put out his hand to his erstwhile employer. Carey reciprocated with a shamefaced grimace.

"Good luck, Billy. You'll be all right. You'll get a new place somewhere, you'll see."

The words were meaningless, empty. Both of them knew that Billy would never get another circus job. There were only a couple of shows on the road as it was, and they were staffed by young, pushy European artistes who travelled the world from season to season, had specialized highly polished acts. High wire people, animal trainers, bareback riders, all still contributed to the heady atmosphere of the sawdust ring but clowning wasn't what it used to be. There were still a few on the payrolls of course, they were needed as fillers between the different routines but most of them were old timers like Billy Duffy. The young people didn't have the interest any more. They wanted the well paying jobs, the slick, colourful, thrilling stunts that resonated with awed audiences who never ceased to be mesmerised by the romance and breath taking presentations that they had come to see.

Billy went back to his caravan and sat down heavily on one of the cushioned benches that doubled up as bunks at night. The trailer belonged to the circus. It had been his home for years. It went with the job, but now he would have to give it up. He got a bottle of whiskey from a cupboard and poured himself a glass. He splashed in some bottled water and ruefully considered his position. The circus would want the caravan immediately. It was no use to Billy. He had no way of towing it even if Carey had been prepared to give it to him. One of the roustabouts would get it. The van wasn't grand enough for any of the other artistes. Billy had been content with it because it was familiar, part of a familiar life which had now come to a sudden and unexpected end.

Billy knew that his days as a professional funnyman would have to end sometime but he had hoped to die in harness supported by the camaraderie of circus life, the friendly banter, the cheerfulness a special people inured to hardship, the security of knowing that there would always be some sort of a job around the Big Top. But things had changed. The circus had always been a tough business, dependant on a fickle public for survival, but it had looked after its own. Now that was changed too. Management had no room for sentiment. If

LAUGHTER

you were no longer useful you were out.

Billy sighed, swallowed the rest of his whiskey and rummaged in a cupboard for a hold all. His possessions were few. He could carry what he had, clothes, old photographs, a couple of books, his clown's suit and face paints. It wasn't much to bring away after a lifetime's work he reflected, but you didn't collect much in a life on the road. But if he had few material things he had a vast portfolio of memories of great times and great performances, of life with very special people, and the smells and sounds of exotic animals which few settled people every encountered.

He heaved his bag up on the flimsy table and went out to make a round of farewells to people he had known for years, others who had only been around for the current season. They were not surprised. Word had got quickly got around that people had been left go. They were sympathetic but phlegmatic, the way they expected Billy himself to be. No emotion, no recriminations, just a casual goodbye and good luck, see you around somewhere.

Saying goodbye to the other clowns was the hardest moment. There had been four clowns on the payroll, Billy's departure would create a void in the routines but they would cover it up. The public would never know. Danny Glover brought him in to his caravan and sat Billy down for a farewell drink. The other two, Harry O'Connor and Johnny Ward, summoned by the telepathy of the showground arrived a few minutes later There wouldn't be much time for farewells. The circus was on the move and the tow trucks would be hitching up to pull the wagons onwards to the next location.

They sat in silence. There was no much to be said, their sympathy expressed by their presence. Billy studied his companions. They were all fairly elderly men, except for Johnny Ward who was still in his forties. None of them were as old as Billy himself and he realized just how far he had traveled along life's pathway. He would be seventy in a few weeks time. He could get the old age pension, he told himself, that would help financially, but first he would need to have a permanent place to stay.

Settling down to old age would be a problem. Life on the road had not been easy, but it had its compensations. There had always been the thrill of the circus to bolster him, the music, the flashing lights, the cracking of the ringmaster's whip, his stentorian announcements, the cheers of the audience, the marvelling faces of the children at the ringside. All that was finished, these men would share the bright, spangled world for a while and then they too would be sent away to live out the rest of their days in solitude.

The conversation strayed over the years that they had worked together, the easy gigs, the calamities, covered up so that no one in the audience could see that mistakes had been made, the good towns, the bad towns, the weather. The weather was always with them. Rain and mud were staples in the constant grind of travelling to new pitches, getting all the caravans and animal wagons on site, stabilising the Big Top against disaster.

They sat together for nearly an hour, four comrades who had spent years of their working life together. Eventually the rap on the trailer door by the truck driver who had come to tow the caravan to its next location broke up this sombre final get together.

Billy shook hands with his mates, a tear glistening in his eye, hefted his bag with its sparse collection of his possessions and set off across the fairground to the town. It was evening now. The street lights were glowing in the first shadows of darkness. He walked quickly, anxious to put the nearly dismantled circus behind him. He was starting out on a new life and the memories of what had gone before were too traumatic. He needed closure and with it the resolution that he should manage the future as deftly as he had made his way successfully through the past.

He walked until he came to a house with a hanging sign that offered bed and breakfast. It would do for tonight, but he would have to get himself a room or a small flat. His money would not last forever, and he would need a permanent address if he was to claim the old age pension. Old age. That was a stunner. It had crept up on him unawares although he was fully conscious of the fact, when he performed his routines in the ring, that he was not as lithe or supple as had once been. Now he was finished, an old man cast off from the security of a long held job, left to fend for himself in a world which was not really his own. The circus had been a mantle, protecting him from the ravages of a life outside, a life to which would now have to adapt, to submit to a daily roster of old man's activities where once he had travelled the country, spreading happiness and laughter to every town in Ireland.

A grey haired woman opened the door, scrutinized him closely and said that she had a room for him. She brought him upstairs to a pleasant bedroom overlooking the street and offered him a cup of tea. He accepted gratefully. The whiskey had dulled his senses slightly and he was glad of the hot cup of tea. He needed to think out a plan of campaign and a clear head was necessary for this.

He pulled out the envelope that Chris Carey had given him and counted the notes onto the bed. Carey had been generous enough given that he was in trouble financially. There was six weeks ages in the envelope, enough to allow him to pay a deposit on a flat and have some eating money over. He would have to go to the Social Welfare office in the morning and get things moving on drawing his pension. Carey's money would last only a few weeks and he would need something extra pretty soon.

The night passed fitfully. The bed was comfortable but he missed his caravan bunk bed and the trailer's familiar undulating movement from the breeze. After a lifetime spent in varied roady sleeping accommodations, Billy found the steadiness of the room disturbing. The house was on a quiet street and he missed the night sounds of the sleeping circus, the creaking of the animals cages, the whipping of the wind in the Big Top's canvas.

Next morning's breakfast, a full fry, was a novelty for Billy. He seldom had more than a cup of coffee at breakfast time. Cooking was not one of his accomplishments and for years he had paid one of the animal trainer's wives to rustle him up some food each evening. From here on he would have to do his own cooking unless he found himself in a boarding house. That was the second of his preferred options. Billy liked his own company, preferred to live an unregimented life, and knew that he would find lodgings with a family difficult. Regular meal times were anathema as was any kind of discipline. Billy was his own man and intended to live out the remainder of his life as he had done in the past, in control, subject to no one, an independent man with a record of solid achievement behind him.

After breakfast he went for a walk around the town. A call to the local newspaper office provided him with a list of flats to let, and he viewed one or two. They were dingy and unwelcoming, not that Billy was used to any great style. His caravan had been shabby, well used, the furnishings battered and the carpet trampled with years of ingrained mud from a thousand different pitches. After several tries he finally found what he wanted, a bright airy bed sitter with its own bathroom and kitchenette. The rent was reasonable, he had enough for the security deposit, and he moved in a few hours later.

LAUGHTER

It wasn't much of a removal. He had a couple of dog eared photographs of himself in his clown costume, and another large print of the circus ring full of animals and performers, the ringmaster resplendent in top hat, riding boots and tailcoat. The photographs were simple yet effective reminders of what his life had been.

He went for walk suddenly conscious of a familiar scringe of pain in his right hip. He eased a hand down his leg, grimaced, and wondered if he would someday need a hip operation. A lifetime's tumbling had certainly taken its toll, but it was only in recent months that he had felt any discomfort. Stiffness was a part of him now and the knuckles on his hands were beginning to swell. While he resented Chris Carey's decision to pay him off in his heart he realized that it really was time to quit. Clowning in the circus was hard physical work. Even if Carey had been agreeable, Billy knew that his days in the sawdust ring would have been numbered. Still, he could have worked on, cleaning up, helping out in the box office, doing lighter jobs showing people to their seats. Once the circus had girls in spangled tights to act as stewards, but that too had been an expence that could not be sustained and young roustabouts now acted as seating stewards.

He was walking, mulling things over in his mind, when a girl on a bicycle approached in the opposite direction. She was young probably about nine or ten, and she exhibited the careless vigour which Billy now so obviously lacked. She was careless too weaving in and out of traffic with the contemptuous familiarity which the young so often exhibit in dangerous situations.

Billy was aware of her peril before the accident. A car came out of a side street and crashed into her, the driver recognizing the danger and applying his brakes to come to a screeching halt. But it was too late. The girl and her bicycle were spreadeagled on the street. Billy rushed to her aid, and a small crowd gathered. The car driver got out of his vehicle and stood there, white faced, trying to convince anyone who would listen that it was not his fault. It wasn't either. He might have been going a bit fast for the place that he was in, but it was the girl who had been at fault. She had been swinging along, totally unconcerned and oblivious to what was going on around her. It was one of countless traffic minor accidents which happened every day in every town in the country.

Billy took off his jacket and put it under the girl's head. She was conscious, moaning, crying out that her leg was broken. And so it was. Billy had seen his share of accidents in the circus, some of them quite serious when people had fallen from the wire, or a rider had slipped off a cantering horse. He took the girl's hand in his and murmured some consoling words. There was little that he could say. The girl was hurt, in pain and words alone would not bring any mind of consolation.

An ambulance came and the professionals took over. Reluctantly the girl let go of Billy's hand. He asked her name and she murmured a response. He leaned forward to hear her words but was elbowed aside by one of the paramedics. He thought she said Monica and repeated this. She smiled a wan response, her features suddenly diffused with pain as one of the ambulance men bound a temporary splint to her leg.

"Where do you live," Billy asked urgently. "I'll tell your parents what happened.

She murmured an address and again Billy leaned forward to catch what she said. She repeated it, and satisfied that he had got it correctly, he stood up and let the ambulance men have more room. Finally satisfied that they had got their patient temporarily stabilized, they lifted the stretcher and brought it to the ambulance. Moments later they were gone, the siren screaming and blue lights flashing.

LAUGHTER

Billy asked directions to the girl's house and hurried down the street. It wasn't far away. Monica's father answered the doorbell, listened to what Billy had to say, and went back inside to get his wife. A small girl, younger than Monica came to the door and peered shyly up at Billy. He tousled her hair and waited until both parents came back to the door. They were naturally alarmed and Billy tried to reassure them that it wasn't too serious. Monica had some injuries he said but she was conscious and in no danger. The main thing was that her leg seemed to be broken.

Both parents pulled on some outdoor clothes and left to go to the hospital bringing their youngest daughter with them. Billy went back to his flat disturbed and unsettled by what had happened, but conscious that he had done the right thing. His instincts to care for children, honed by his long years of clowning had come to the fore. He had been a minor ministering angel in a time of crisis for a little girl and her family.

He went to the hospital the following day. Monica was in the children's ward, her leg encased in plaster but otherwise seemingly little affected by her experience. She recognized Billy from he scene of the accident and told him that she was in some pain but was taking tablets for this, she explained, Billy gave her some sweets he had bought and sat down to talk to her for a few moments. The ward was full of children, all of them suffering in some way, but some not as sick as others. The nurses had put up posters and drawings on the walls and there were stocks of cuddly toys, and games.

Billy counted the beds. There were twenty in altogether, all of them occupied, some by children who could get up, others by still, silent forms, their situations obviously more critical. Billy did some pocket magic for the children who were out of bed, beamed at the sounds of awe and amazement, and after an hour or so said goodbye to Monica and her newfound friends.

He went back to his flat in a thoughtful frame of mind. There were children everywhere in the world, he mused, not just around the ringside at the circus. He opened his make-up box and began to paint his face. After half an hour or so he was satisfied and changed into his clown's costume. He let himself out into the street and walked towards the hospital. People smiled at him and offered cheery greetings. Billy smiled back and waved. It was a carefree day and he was in his working uniform. The very sight of him, a bizarre and memory conjuring figure amongst the everyday pedestrians and car drivers created its own special magic. The clown was in the streets, it would be a happy day.

At the hospital he was greeted with rapturous enthusiasm. He sang and danced and did his pocket magic, producing flowers and multicoloured handkerchiefs, and coins from behind children's ears. Nurses and parents gathered in the ward to watch the show and clapped and cheered along with their children. Billy clapped his hands together in appreciation of their applause and gave a final bow. There were calls for encores and he obliged, eventually concluding with the promise that he would be back again. And so he would. Clowning would not be left behind at the circus. There were other audiences, other children to enthuse and entertain. A clown's life could go on for ever.

Loss

"My daughter is missing."

It was the first time that she had said the words. Somehow she felt that it was her only acknowledgement that something was wrong. Up until that moment she had refused to accept that things were not right, that the terrible feeling of despair which engulfed her was somehow not real, a passing fixation, and that Emma would come into the house, rushing home from school to change and get to her part time job in the local supermarket.

But Emma had not come home, and now Mary was revealing her dread to an expressionless policeman, who stared at her with no apparent indication that he understood what she was saying.

"It's been two days," Mary said in a louder voice, determined to get some reaction, some indication that her fears were communicable and that something would be done.

"She didn't come home from school on Tuesday afternoon," she went on. "I've heard nothing. There's been no sign of her. I asked around, her friends, the teachers at the school. Nobody has seen her."

The policeman, he was a sergeant, asked her name. She gave it. Mary Fowler. He wrote down her address and the last time that she had seen Emma.

"It might not be too serious," the sergeant said in an attempt to reassure her. "She might have run off with a boyfriend. Teenagers do that you know. They soon come back when they run out of money. We get a lot of that. She'll turn up. They always do."

"I want a search," Mary said desperately, appalled by this

apparent attempt to attempt to brush off her fears. "She's never done this before. She doesn't have a boy friend, not a steady one at any rate."

"They all have boy friends," the sergeant said. "Even the youngest ones. You'll find she's holed up somewhere in a boarding house, or a hotel. She'll be back in a day or two"

"She hasn't any money," Mary rejoined a trace of anger in her voice. She was becoming impatient at the sergeant's list of excuses. In her distraught state it felt as if he was trying every avenue to avoid taking action.

The sergeant sighed and went across the office to get another piece of paper. He brought it back and pushed it across the counter to Mary. It was headed Missing Person Report, and had a string of questions. Names, addresses, dates, age last time of sighting, description, height, clothes. Mary painstakingly filled in the answer to every question and handed the form back to the policeman. He scrutinized it, satisfied himself that she had not left anything out and put it in a folder.

"This makes it official," he said in a more kindly tone. "Go back home and wait. We'll put out a description of your daughter. The area car will keep a look out. Try not to worry. She'll be back soon enough."

Mary left the police station, slightly relieved now that she had done something positive about finding Emma. The feeling of dread was still there, however, and the sergeant's well meant words of reassurance had done nothing for her.

She went home and busied herself around the house for a while, then went upstairs to Emma's room. It was in its characteristically untidy state, clothes on the floor, the bed unmade, books and discs strewn across the dressing table.

LOSS

There were photographs of school friends, all girls, and a large framed portrait of her father, another picture pinned to the wall was of the three of them, taken in the days when Gerry was still at home, before he had decided to take off for God knows where leaving his wife and daughter to fend for themselves.

It had not been easy bringing up Emma on her own. The preschool stage had been the hardest period. Neighbours and her mother had helped out with baby sitting allowing Mary to work in a local solicitor's office as a typist. It was easier when Emma went to school. There wasn't the same pressure, and as she reached her mid teenage years, Emma herself did part time work, giving a share to her mother for housekeeping and spending the remainder on the things that teenage girls could not do without.

Mary sat down on the bed and sobbed for a few moments. She had never felt so lonely, not even when Gerry had left. She was afraid, afraid for herself, afraid for Emma. Someday she knew Emma would leave, either to get married or to live with someone. It was the fashion nowadays. Young people didn't get married any more. They just got together, set themselves up in flats and parted when they felt they were in need of a change of partner.

Emma had been a good girl by and large. There had been episodes of drinking, late nights with her friends, surreptitious smoking, but she had caused Mary very little grief over the years. Until now that was. Two days missing without a phone call. She had never stayed away from home before. It was most unlike her. Mary dialed Emma's mobile again, as she had been doing regularly since her daughter had failed to come home on Tuesday evening but it was still powered off. Emma had bought the phone out of her shop money and it had become one of her most treasured possessions, always in use taking or receiving calls or texts. Mary was certain that these were all from other girls. Emma had yet to have a steady

97

boyfriend, one or two from school had come around, but these were sporadic visits, there was no lasting liaison. The sergeant's suggestion that Emma had run off with a boyfriend was extremely unlikely.

On an impulse Mary switched on the computer and checked Emma's e-mail. The computer was a mystery to Mary but Emma had shown her the basics. There were several incoming e-mails, most of them junk mail. There was nothing on Emma's list of personal contacts. She switched off again and lay back on the bed, her sense of dread increased. She felt ill, unusually tired, completely overwhelmed with a numbing sense of fear. She went downstairs again and made some tea. Sitting at the kitchen table she allowed herself to be overcome with black despair. Emma was gone. She was not going to return. The thought kept coursing through her mind. There was no reassurance. No uplifting moment of confidence that would dispel her desolation.

A knock came to the door. It was a detective pursuing further information. The interlude was welcome. By talking about Emma, imparting the details of the hours prior to her departure, Mary could keep her despair at bay. The detective listened carefully, made some notes and attempted a note of reassurance.

"Most young people who go off like this turn up after a few days," he said in a comforting tone. "I don't think there is anything to worry about. She'll turn up. They always do."

Mary almost screamed out her disgust at the comforting formula. It wasn't what she wanted to hear. They didn't understand. Emma was gone. Something terrible had occurred. She wasn't going to turn up in a day or so.

"I want a search made," she said. "People should be out looking for her. She might be ill, have been in an accident, fallen into the river, anything."

"We've checked the hospitals," the detective said. "There's no one there. I'm certain she's gone off with a boyfriend for a few days. It happens. The parents are usually the last ones to know."

Mary rapped her fist on the table.

"I know," she said. "She hasn't run away. Something has happened."

"Did you have a fight before she disappeared," the detective asked. "Any ill feeling. Any harsh words. It happens. Some kids take things very seriously."

Again Mary rapped her hands on the table.

"Nothing like that," she replied irritably. "We had no falling out whatsoever."

"We need to know the names of her boyfriends." The detective moved in a different direction. "We'll check with all of them. Some of the other young people will have information, I'm sure of that."

"She doesn't have a steady boyfriend," Mary answered. "She wasn't really into that. I went through all this with the sergeant this morning."

Reluctantly she gave the detective the names of one or two young lads who had come around in the past. He got the names of girl friends as well, writing down the information in a notebook that seemed to have more loose pages than fixed sheets.

"We'll go round to the school," he said. "We're sure to pick up something there. These kind of secrets always get out. Someone knows something. You'll see."

With that he left, satisfied that he had gone through the motions, oblivious of the fact that he had provided Mary with no support or consolation at all.

She sat around for awhile, waiting for the telephone to ring, but it was silent. Part of her wanted to go out and search the lanes, stands of timber and riverbank at the edge of the town, but she was torn between this and staying in, hoping that Emma would ring and all her fears would be dispelled. She mustn't be out when Emma rang.

But Emma didn't ring. The police telephoned around teatime to find out if she had heard anything. She clung on to the phone, desperately keeping him talking in the hope that he would come up with something concrete, but eventually the detective, conscious of the fact that he was acting as a sounding board for Mary's trauma, rang off.

"Women" he told the sergeant feelingly as he put down the phone, "they're very easily worked up."

"Kids have no conscience, no sense of responsibility," the sergeant rejoined. "They never think about the trouble they cause, or what they put their parents through."

The detective nodded disinterestedly. His shift was coming to an end and he had things to do. His own kids were grown up and away working. He was glad. The joys of parenthood began to pall after they reached a certain age. They became adults and had to look out for themselves. Still he wasn't unsympathetic to Mary's trouble. But she should be more realistic, he told himself. Too many mothers lived in a kind of shell, cocooned from reality, refusing to admit that their daughters became young women at a very early stage and that they were into drugs and sex. Parents need to catch themselves on. The world had changed. Their offspring fled the nest earlier and engaged in pursuits that their parents in their own teenage years had never contemplated.

Finally Mary could stick the house no longer. The phone wasn't going to ring and she needed to take some positive action. A visit to Emma's closest friend, Angela, seemed a logical and progressive thing to do. She put on a coat and hurried round to Angela's house. Her mother answered the door and brought Mary in. She called up to Angela's bedroom and the girl came down. A quick flash of apprehension crossed her face, but Angela was adamant that she knew nothing. Emma had given no indication that she was going to take off anywhere, and she knew of no one in whose company she might be found. Mary cross examined the girl, the same age as Emma but there was no further information forthcoming. She sighed and leaned back in her chair, tears not far away. Angela's mother brought some tea and the three of them conversed in muted tones. Mary resumed her cross examination but it produced no further information. Emma had last been seen by Angela at school the day she had disappeared. She had given no indication that anything was wrong. She had walked out of school and vanished.

Something niggled at Mary. Angela had apparently been forthcoming but an uneasiness persisted. Somehow Mary got the feeling that Angela was holding something back. She couldn't put her finger on it and it was clear that further questioning was pointless. Whatever nugget of information Angela was withholding, it wasn't going to be shared.

Mary left and walked to the outskirts of town. There was a path through the woods and she followed it aimlessly. Could Emma have gone this way. Had she gone to the river and fallen in, drowned. Mary sobbed to herself as the awful picture

101

imprinted itself on her mind. Emma dying a lonely death in the polluted stream, no one to hear her cries. She walked on to the river bank and wandered along for a mile or more. The river seemed peaceful, green algae at the edge apparently undisturbed. If Emma had fallen in surely there would have been some trace, some sign at the place where she had been engulfed. Try as she could, Mary could make no sense of her thoughts. If Emma was in the river she had made no mark at her point of entrance.

Mary went back to the house and disconsolately switched on the television to hear the news. Not that she thought that there would be anything about Emma in the broadcast. The police would surely know before the news people she surmised and they would have been round to give her whatever information they had. No news was good news, she reflected. If anything had happened to Emma her body would have been found by now. Perhaps it was true what the police were saying. That she had run off with someone. If that was the case, she would get in touch eventually. Emma was a dutiful and loving daughter. She would not keep her mother in agonized suspence for too long.

Nothing happened for two more days, but finally the detective returned. They had come up with a boy's name they told her. One of Emma's school friends had suggested a link. The boy was also missing, although his parents had not reported this. He had gone away on many previous occasions and they saw nothing unusual in his current absence or didn't particularly care.

Mary was overjoyed. Emma was alive. It was only a matter of time before she made contact. A great burden had been lifted from her and she got back into her usual routine. Gone were the long silences, the hours and hours of staring into nothingness, the pain and dread that Emma would be found dead or drowned. Word of the changed situation soon got out and neighbours called with their good wishes. Everyone was pleased for her. No one wanted a lost child in their midst.

Now Mary knew what Angela had been trying to keep from her. The quick flash of fear that had crossed the face of her daughter's friend still remained with Mary. Angela had known all this but had wanted to keep the secret. Mary was annoyed but this was soon dissipated with the exultation that this good news had brought in its wake. Angela could keep her secret but it would have no effect on the march of events. Emma would be found, would be back at home in a very short space of time, she was sure.

Mary's joy was tempered to some extent by the fact that Emma had gone away without a word in the first place, that she had been so heartless as to not even make a reassuring telephone call. But the important thing was that nothing serious had befallen here. She was in the whirlwind of a teenage romance. Mary could empathise with this. Emma had always been strong willed but highly emotional. She felt things keenly, and her first foray into adult love was bound to be spectacular. The days, however, drew on, and there was no word.

Unable to restrain her self any further, Mary went round to the boy's parents. His name was Jimmy Murphy and they lived about a mile away. She wasn't well received. There had been a lot of unwanted speculation about their son and Emma and they resented the fact that they had suddenly become notorious. Their son was difficult, always in trouble, and this latest escapade with a local girl was another instance of the problems he caused them. Mary was kept on the doorstep. Clearly there was to be no bonding between the two families. Emma's association with their son was an irritant. The pair would come home eventually and the escapade would be shelved as just another instance of the trouble that their son caused for his parents. Mary resented their attitude. They clearly were not interested in taking any responsibility for their son's actions and her daughter was being treated as an unwanted participant in Jimmy's misbehaviour.

Mary went back home in an angry frame of mind. She was outraged at the attitude adopted by Jimmy's parents. They had been casual, totally indifferent to the agony that she had gone through. She couldn't understand why they didn't have the same concerns about Jimmy. He was their son, surely they loved him, and wanted to know that he was safe. The detective called around the following morning and she confided her thoughts to him. He was non committal. He had encountered Jimmy Murphy on several occasions and had him before the Children's Court for various misdemeanours.

"He's a bit wild," he told Mary. "The parents have had a lot of trouble with him. He's out of control. There's nothing they can do about him."

Mary's relief that Emma, if not found, was certainly no longer lying dead in the countryside, was turning to anger. How could she be so heartless. How could she jeopardize her mother's love for the casual fumblings of a discontented teenage boy. Now that she knew what had happened to Emma she wanted her found, brought home, her association with Jimmy Murphy terminated.

"We think they're in Dublin," the detective confided. "Jimmy was talking about going to the city. Some of his schoolmates knew. We've sent their description to headquarters. They'll notify all the city police stations. It's only a matter of time until they're picked up."

"What are they using for money," Mary asked. "Emma had nothing, only a few euro coins. They'll need money to live on."

"Jimmy didn't have much either," the detective admitted. "They might be staying with someone they know, but if they're not they'll need money for lodgings and food. That's a bit of a mystery, but Jimmy Murphy won't be stuck. He'll find someway of getting hold of cash."

He didn't tell Mary that on past form, Jimmy's approach to getting hold of cash would be illegal. Shoplifting, even outright robbery would not be beyond his capabilities. If that was the case Emma would be implicated. Both of them could be charged and brought before the courts.

Mary understood the drift of his conversation. Emma had fallen in with a bad lot and could be damaged by this association.

"I want her back" she told the detective feelingly. "Now that you know who she's with you should be able to find them."

"It's not that easy," the detective said. "But the Superintendent is concerned that Emma is only sixteen. Murphy is a year older. He can look after himself. We'll do our best to find them, but it will take time. In the meantime stay near the phone and hope that she rings in."

With that he was gone, a busy man with more things on his schedule than a runaway teenage couple. The threat of something worse befalling Emma had been lifted with the realization that she was only a runaway, no longer a child who had totally vanished without trace.

The good news was dulled as a few more days passed without any word from Emma or indication by the police that they had caught up with the runaway couple. Mary's relief turned to annoyance. How could Emma do this to her. Mary had been a loving mother and she believed that they had a loving relationship. Now all that was destroyed by Emma's coldness, by the sheer lack of concern for her mother. A phone call was all that was needed, but it was not forthcoming.

Then the detective returned. This time he was accompanied by a woman police officer.

"I've bad news," he said sombrely as they sat in the front room. "We've traced Jimmy Murphy. He was staying in a flat in Dublin with a couple of other young men. But Emma isn't with him. He denies any knowledge of her and is adamant that he left home alone. He has no relationship with your daughter whatsoever. His story is backed by his companions. Emma and Jimmy Murphy were never together."

Mary listened to him with a sinking heart. Her relief with the belief that her daughter was safe even if she was in the hands of a tearaway, had been totally misplaced.

"Are you sure," she asked the detective. "Perhaps he's lying. Perhaps Emma went with him and left to go somewhere else."

The detective shook his head. "We're satisfied that she was never with him," he said. "We've checked it all out. Wherever Emma went it wasn't in the company of Jimmy Murphy."

Mary began to cry. All her hopes had been dashed. It was bad enough that Emma had left home to go with a teenage hooligan but now even that slender hope had been dashed. Where was Emma. What had happened to her. She buried her face in her hands and began to sob uncontrollably. The agony had begun all over again.

The policewoman got up and went to the kitchen to make some tea. Mary wiped her eyes and looked appealingly at the detective. He was uncomfortable, unable to withstand the sheer desolation that had so suddenly affected Mary. Emma had been missing for weeks. The false hopes that had been raised when Jimmy Murphy too had left home dashed utterly.

"We've wasted a lot of time," the policeman admitted. "The Superintendent is very concerned. We're carrying out a search of all the surrounding countryside, but we want you to make an appeal on television. The Superintendent thinks that someone might come forward if we get some publicity."

Mary nodded miserably. The feeling of disaster affected her once again, a terrible chill of fear. Emma had been gone for weeks. Something awful had happened to her. Now she was beginning to believe that she would never see her daughter again.

The detective adopted an air of forced cheerfulness.

"Don't give up hope," he said consolingly. "She has to be somewhere. We'll find her eventually."

The broadcast appeal was rushed forward. The police brought Mary to the station and the cameras were set up in a conference room. The Superintendent came in to meet Mary and assure her that they were doing everything possible. The appeal would bring a result he was sure. Emma or someone close to her would be sure to see it. Mary's ordeal would be over in a matter of hours.

Mary felt that he was striving to be more confident than he really felt. If Emma was alright she would have been in touch by now. She clutched at a faint straw of hope. Perhaps Emma was with another boy. Perhaps there was someone that the police didn't know about.

The television people made a couple of takes to get the message right on target. Mary got through it without breaking down. It was important that she connected well with her daughter. A wailing heap of misery on television was not the image she wanted to project. There were telephone calls after the broadcast which went out on the six o'clock news. Sightings were reported from all over the country, but every one of them turned out to be a dead end. Some of the phone calls were malicious, one woman said that Mary deserved all her trouble for failing to bring up her daughter properly. Other calls were from people who genuinely felt that they had seen Emma somewhere. Many calls were simply from people who wanted to convey their sympathy and good wishes. But there was no hard lead to Emma and the police pronounced themselves baffled.

A widespread and detailed search of the fields, woods and wasteland outside the town was conducted without result. The river was dragged. Hundreds of people went out to help the police. Soldiers were brought in from the Army barracks at Athlone, the police helicopter made dozens of sweeps over the terrain but the final result was nothing. Emma had disappeared as completely as if she had never existed.

As every long and tortuous day drew to a close without and development, Mary sank into deeper depression. She began to blame herself for not looking after Emma better, the occasions when they had minor rows returned to her magnified and even more distressing. The police came to the house every couple of days, but they had nothing to report. Mary went to the doctor and was prescribed anti-depressants, the physician kind and understanding, but determined that she should take as little medication as possible. He was not prepared to over prescribe. Mary listened, took the prescription to the chemist and went back home. There were plenty of phone calls from well wishers, some from cranks. But none brought the news that she so desperately wanted to hear.

She reviewed every moment of the days before Emma had

gone away. There was no clue there. Emma had vanished without a trace, without a hint of what she was going to do. Someone had to know, Mary thought desperately. Someone out there who was callous enough to ignore the every plea for information could still hold the key that would resolve Mary's terrible agony.

Angela came into her mind. For some reason she couldn't get rid of a feeling that the girl knew something. There had been the quick flash of anxiety when Mary had come to the door that day. Angela was the one person that Emma would have confided in. The girl had held something back that day. It was time for the truth to come out.

Mary went round to Angela's house right away. Her mother wasn't too pleased to see her but let her in and called for her daughter to come down from her room. This time Mary was forceful, domineering even. No longer was there any reason to tread diffidently. If Angela knew anything Mary was determined to extract it.

Angela's mother stayed in the room, but Mary ploughed in without any preliminaries.

"I want you to tell me the truth," she exhorted. "You know something. Where is Emma. Tell me, tell me."

Angela looked at her mother and started to cry.

Concerned at Angela's sudden breakdown, her mother tried to intervene, but Mary was having none of it.

"She knows something," she insisted. "I want the truth. Now. Tell me about Emma."

Angela wiped her eyes and looked sulkily at her mother.   She

109

didn't want to talk. But Mary was determined that the truth would have to be told. Finally Angela realized that she could withstand the situation no longer.

"Emma was having a relationship with an older man" the girl said, snivelling into a tissue. "It was all highly secret. I won't know who he was but it was very intense."

"An older man," Mary echoed. "What man."

"I don't know" the girl answered. "She was very secretive about the whole thing. She knew that you wouldn't approve, but she was very much in love."

Mary's mouth tightened in derision. What did these young girls know about love.

"Was it someone from the town," Mary asked. "Tell me."

"I don't know who it was," the girl answered sobbing again.

The girl's mother intervened, but half heartedly. She looked shocked. Her daughter had withheld vital information about someone for whom the whole countryside had been turned upside down.

"Are you sure you don't know who it is," her mother asked. Angela ran across the room and pushed herself into her mother's arms."

"I don't know anything more," she cried. "She wouldn't tell me. I just know that it was an older man and that he had made her say nothing to anyone."

Satisfied that she had elicited everything from the distraught girl, Mary left and went down to the police station. The detective brought her into an interview room and she recounted everything that Angela had told her. He was grave faced. They would interview Angela for themselves, he told her. This new development would be processed and the police would direct their inquiries at men who were known to target young girls.

"Where is she," Mary demanded catching his arm in a gesture which expressed her alarm and terrible fear. "What has happened to her."

The detective made a few comforting remarks and went off to consult with the Superintendent. Both men came back into the room, both equally serious. This was not good news, but they couldn't say this to Mary. Sporadic encounters between teenagers and older men were not uncommon, but what was so deeply disturbing was the fact that no trace of Emma had been found. It increasingly looked as if Emma would not be found alive. It was now nearly six weeks since she had disappeared. It was unlikely that any relationship with a young girl would have lasted this long. Older men had their own lives to live. Close contact with an immature teenager would begin to pall. They would have commitments. They were unlikely to spend such a long time away from home.

The police moved quickly. Angela was interviewed and a short list of suspects was drawn up. By the end of the next day all of these had been interviewed. They were no further forward. No one had admitted seeing Emma and all could account for their movements in the days after she had disappeared. Despite the appearance of candour, however, the detective was certain that one man was holding something back. Years of experience in the force had given the policeman an edge when it came to interviewing suspects. He could tell when he was being told a lie. One of these men was lying, he was certain, but there was no apparent way of proceeding any further.

He called to Mary and outlined the situation. They had a suspect in mind but unless he confessed there was very little they could do. They would proceed with inquiries to see if any shred of contact with Emma could be unearthed, but even at this comparatively early stage it seemed unlikely that any link would be found.

Mary digested all this in silence. She asked for the man's name but the detective withheld it. That information was confidential, he told her. They might be wrong about this man, and they couldn't risk Mary starting any kind of solo run. She would have to stay away from this until such time as the police could harden up their suspicions.

But nothing concrete came to light. They brought the man down to the police station on two occasions and conducted relentless interviews, but he denied knowing Emma or having anything to do with her. Reluctantly they had to let him go. Mary found out his identity for herself within a few days. News travels fast in a small town and everyone was stirred up by the never ending drama of Emma's disappearance.

Mary walked past his house two or three times before she could find enough courage to tackle him for herself. He came to the door, a tall heavily built man in his middle thirties, dressed casually in jeans and a sweater and scuffed trainers. Mary wondered what Emma could see in him. He certainly wasn't at all attractive as far as she could see.

He was belligerent, clearly fully conscious of the fact that he was the subject of town gossip. Not a nice man, Mary decided, although he was good looking in an overweight kind of way. After her first few halting words of introduction he stepped back and slammed the door in her face. She made some inquiries amongst his neighbours. He was married with one child, and had been involved with an altercation with his wife some months ago that had resulted in someone living nearby sending for the police. Apart from this nothing much was known about him.

Mary went home dis-satisfied but unable to progress the situation any further. The man wouldn't speak to her but in any event had apparently been cleared for the time being by the police. There was nothing to link him with Emma apart from the detective's gut feeling that this was their man. But there was no evidence and they could do nothing more.

The search in the countryside outside the town was widened. This time the searchers were looking for a body although they kept this information from Mary. But despite all the efforts nothing was found. Emma had vanished without trace. It was a mystery which apparently was incapable of solution.

The weeks drifted into months and Mary although she never grew accustomed to the fact that she was alone in the house, slowly began to adjust to the reality that Emma was gone. The telephone rang less, people ceased to commiserate with her and the visits from the detective became fewer and fewer until they stopped altogether. Gradually she became accustomed to her loss, but still she never gave up hope that someday Emma would come back. It was a forlorn hope, but nonetheless a tiny flicker of expectancy that would sustain her in the years that lay ahead. Once she had a beautiful daughter who had one day walked out of her life never to be seen again. Mary's wound would never heal. Somewhere out there someone had a secret. Until the silence was broken Mary would wait, uncomplainingly now, but nonetheless committed to the belief that someday Emma would return. Someday...

Greed

"The Department people are at Willie Dempsey's place."

Anna rushed into the kitchen where her husband Tom Foley was having his mid morning cup of tea. Tom was unmoved. She tried to stir him once more.

"They're counting the sheep. It's an inspection. They're going to do all the farms. It's about the subsidy. They think that we have all been claiming for sheep that we don't own."

This time Tom Foley showed some concern.

"They can't count the sheep on everyone's place. Most of them are on the mountain. They'd never get around."

Anna shook her head in exasperation.

"They're making Willie bring them all down. There's five or six inspectors. They say they're going to check every ewe in the valley."

Sheep had been Tom Foley's way of life for decades. His father and grandfather had been sheep men and they were steeped in knowledge. The home place was only thirty acres but the mountains which rose up behind their tiny farm offered commonage and thousands upon thousands of acres of additional grazing even if some of it was very sparse indeed. The subsidy cheque had been the family's main support for several years. There was not enough money in raising sheep without it. There was not enough money in any branch of farming these days, but if you were a small farmer on the mountain times were tough indeed.

The Black Valley was an isolated withdrawn place cut off from the rest of the county by its ring of mountains and accessible by means of only one major road.   There were side

roads, of course, but only the valley people used these.
Strangers coming in, tourists, traveling sales men, insurance
agents and the like stuck to the main road. The Valley and is
mountain hinterland were indescribably beautiful, but it was
notoriously difficult to traverse. The inhabitants, all of them
small farmers wrenching a living from their bleak holdings
and all of them dependent on sheep and the Department's
cheque for that living, were inhospitable, clannish, very much
their own people. They had not interest in outsiders, whoever
they were. This had been the way for generations. Life in
many ways had passed them by but all were agreed, they stuck
to this place because their fathers had done so. It was harsh,
bleak, uninviting, but it was home.

The nature of the place had made its people tough and
calculating. Every shilling they earned had to be hacked from
the hinterland, every lamb that came into the world was a
bonus, every one that was lost a minor disaster. Foley walked
to the door of his cottage and looked out towards Willie
Dempsey's place. There was some activity alright. He could
hear the whistles as Willie sent his dogs after the sheep in the
small stonewalled fields near the house, and there were cars
parked in the front yard.

A twinge of uneasiness tugged at him. How could they count
the sheep. It wasn't possible, Most of the flocks were out on
the mountain. It would be a major job to bring them down.
Surely the Department men would not have the patience for
this. He swore angrily. Interfering bastards. Did they think
they could outwit folk who had been living on their wits for
hundreds of years. This was the Black Valley. There was a
time when no one ventured into its inhospitable hillsides. They
had some cheek coming here.

He watched the activity at Dempsey's for awhile and looked
up at the hillside where his own flock were grazing. The sheep
knew their own pastures, they didn't mix with the flocks of the

other sheepmen, each flock had its territory. Like the men who ran them the sheep had bloodlines going back for hundreds of years. They were born to the mountain, knew every crevasse, could find their way to every reluctant blade of grass that forced itself out from amongst the heather.

Tom had a second farm, forty five acres of better land near the mouth of the valley. His brother Michael, a teacher lived in the farmhouse and minded over twenty dry stock, big boned part bred Charolais. These two were slow earners and margins had been getting progressively tighter in recent years. Tom had decided some time ago that there was very little hope for farming, but as long as the cheques kept coming from the Department there was some sort of a living to be made. Many of the farmers in the valley had second jobs, travelling out every morning to factories in the town and bringing home that bit of extra money that made life bearable for men with families.

Tom Foley despised these hybrid sons of the mountain. They were deserters who couldn't cut it on the slopes any more. Some of them had even given up their sheep altogether. Tom didn't care. It left more grazing for those who stuck with the job. Willie Dempsey and Tom were kindred spirits. They lived for their craggy mountain homes, their flocks, their slow lifestyle. Tom realized that his two sons would look for another way of life outside the valley. The small farm wouldn't support them. Tom was there because he had always been there and was content with the way things were. Donal and Malachy would go to college, get degrees and find well paid jobs and security in the outside world. Tom in his heart knew that he was the last of his family who would earn a living from sheep. He didn't mind. The mountain had provided for himself and his family up to now. When he was gone, Anna could sell the place and move into the town. It wasn't much of a legacy but it was something.

GREED

As these thoughts flowed through his mind, his wife came out and stood beside him. Together they looked down at the activity on Willie Dempsey's farm. Willie was on the mountain now whistling at his dogs to bring down the flocks. He would be at least two hours at this. Tom smiled grimly. Willie would be a match for the inspectors. Already he could see that Willie was rounding up some of Tom's sheep as well as his own. The numbers would add up. The inspectors wouldn't know who owned which sheep and they would do their sums in the belief that they were seeing Willie's flock and his alone. Tom and the other farmers would do the same thing when it came to their turn. He knew that there were supposed to be over one hundred thousand sheep in the valley. According to the returns filed with the Department of Agriculture that was. In reality there were only forty thousand, but sheepmen had to make a living. The size of the cheque depended on the size of the herd and for decades the men of the Black Valley had inflated their stock numbers and drawn down their overpayments with impunity.

Tom didn't view this as being dishonest. It was the way things were. The Valley people were condemned to a harsh borderline existence and they were full entitled to anything they could get. It was all about the money. The Minister for Agriculture might have a different view and the accountants in Brussels were not convinced about the stock numbers, but no one would really know the truth. Tom, Willie and the other farmers in the Valley would drive down each others flocks and run them through their yards to produce a tally that would back up each of their claims to the Department. Each man's subsidy would be safe. Tom smiled and took Anna by the arm.

"Come on, we'll go inside. It will be a day or two before they get to us."

As Tom had foreseen it was two days before the inspectors reached Tom's farm.   Word of their presence had spread through the Valley like wildfire and everyone knew the form. Flocks were brought down and recycled time after time. The inspectors had nothing to show for their trouble.

They came on a sunny afternoon. Normally the Valley was shrouded in mist with soft rain falling nearly every day, but this day was bright and cheerful. Tom would have preferred a more miserable afternoon. The inspectors would be less committed if they had to work in the wet, but it would make no difference. Tom listened quietly to what their leader had to say.

"We want your sheep brought down to the home farm," he said. "We're here to do an enumeration. Your subsidy payment next year will depend on what we find."

"I make my returns every year," Tom said mildly.

The other scowled.

"We have reason to believe that things are not what they appear," he said grimly. "We intend to do a thorough check. We expect your co-operation."

"Did you find anything wrong on the other farms," Tom asked maliciously.

The inspector scowled again.

"That's confidential information," he said.

Tom laughed. He knew that nothing out of the way had been found anywhere. The mountainy men were more than a match for these Dublin jackeens who thought that they could march over everyone's land, order them around, and try to cut off the money to which the farmers were entitled. It hadn't happened on anyone else's farm and it wouldn't happen here. Tom

118

would be as good as his neighbours. He would drive down everyone's sheep to make up the numbers and the inspectors would grudgingly note down the results, knowing that they had been hoodwinked but unable to do anything about it.

But this time things were different. Tom brought down the sheep and channeled them through the yard for the Department men to do their tally. Sheep that had been counted several times before ran the gauntlet again, but the inspectors were not as gullible as the mountain men had at first believed. Each sheep was marked with a red die. Tom stared aghast as he saw what was happening. It would be impossible now for the sheep to be produced again. He tried to stop the procedure. He had his neighbours to protect. If these sheep were marked everyone else would come up short. The inspectors would have the proof they needed that the Valley people had been defrauding the Department and drawing down subsidies to which they were not entitled. There would be an investigation and people would have to refund the money. Most of them wouldn't have the resources. Every shilling that came into a house in the Black Valley was spent before each winter was out.

"I don't want any marks on my sheep," Tonm protested. "I have to put my own marks on. This will only confuse things."

The chief inspector smiled his grim smile.

"You can use another dye," he said uncompromisingly. "We're putting on our own marks. We have good reason."

Tom had a problem now. He had only driven in about half the sheep he needed. He wouldn't be able to recycle these again. His tally would come up short. There were other sheep on the mountain of course, but these were too far away. The inspectors would know that they couldn't be his.

119

He went inside to consult with Anna. In times of trouble he turned to her. This time it looked as if big trouble was on the way.

"We're going to be short," he said. "They've marked the sheep and we can't use them again. I could be down over a thousand head."

Anna had no solution. He went outside again. The inspector came up to him.

"Is that all you have, Mr Foley,"he asked sardonically. "Your forms say that you should have a great many more."

Tom was stuck for an answer.

"They must have got lost on the mountain," he said weakly.

The inspector smiled bleakly.

"I don't think so," he said. "You've been caught out. You'll be hearing from us very shortly."

With that he collected his men and they drove off. Thoughtfully Tom opened up the yard gates and released the sheep back into the fields. He would take them to the mountain later on, but in the meantime he had a great deal to think about.

Willie Dempsey came up that evening. Tom filled him in on what had happened. His friend commiserated with him, but had no answers.

"They've got me, the bastards," Tom said feelingly. "I wonder what will happen."

"They've got the whole Valley," Dempsey rejoined. "I was the only one who got away with it. "That inspector is a cute boyo."

The inspections in the Valley continued for another fortnight. Each time a flock was counted it was marked. Every farmer other than Willie Dempsey had been caught in the net. The Department wasted no time in getting to grips with the problem. Letters arrived and each carried the same grim message. The subsidies to the Valley were cut off, refunds had to be made going back for ten years, there would be prosecutions.

Two officials came down from Dublin to talk to Willie Dempsey. He could either admit that he was part of the scam or they were going to count his flock again. Dempsey had no way out. He admitted that he was as guilty as his neighbours and he too received the same threatening letter.

They held a meeting in the region's only hall, a small edifice with a corrugated iron roof, used for occasional dances, whist drives and special gatherings of the community. Seldom had more serious convocation been summoned as that which gathered to discuss the Department's raid and subsequent threats. There were nearly forty farmers present. The debate went on for over two hours with no one coming up with a practicable solution. It seemed that they were destined for the courts, possible jail and serious financial trouble. The subsidies had all been well spent. Even with the plundering of the Department, no one had any spare money left over from one year to the other. It had gone on too long, it had been too easy and they had all been lulled into a false sense of security. The subsidy was like the dole, it came in the post as a right and everyone forgot or conveniently ignored how they had come to claim it in the first place.

It was Willie Dempsey who proposed that they go to the

Farmers Defence Association.

"We can't fight this on our own," he told the meeting. "We need help. The Association will know what to do. They're not going to stand by and let the Department ruin us."

The suggestion was agreed, a delegation was nominated to go to Dublin and enlist the aid of the farmers' organization.

Tom and Willie Dempsey were members of the party. They had an appointment with the President and Secretary of the fifty years old organization which had fought so many battles on behalf of farmers. Tom had reservations. He wasn't sure that they would get a hearing. In his heart he knew that the Valley sheepmen were in the wrong, they had defrauded the Department for years and got away with it. Surely the Association could not be seen to support their activities.

Their reception, however, was warm. The President was up for re-election later in the year and there were votes to be garnered in a campaign for the rights of a downtrodden section of his membership. The Association would demand a meeting with the Minister for Agriculture. The Valley sheepmen would not be alone in their fight for justice.

The Association got its meeting with the minister. It went on for several hours and things became heated. The minister himself was ambivalent, anxious to keep on good terms with the farming community, but his officials were determined that there would be no backing down on the issue. The Valley sheepmen had been caught out in a conspiracy, they had defrauded the state for years and they had to pay the price. It was all about the money.

Tom sat at the back of the room, a feeling of despair gradually supplanting the glimmers of hope that he had entertained when the meeting was first agreed. At first it had looked as if things might go their way. Now the officials were obdurate. They couldn't overlook what had happened. The Minister veered in their direction. He knew that the public wouldn't condone fraud. Farmers were getting too many subsidies as it was. Ordinary workers were paying their taxes to support them. There would be an outcry if this was glossed over.

The FDA President held his ground. The Department could either give way or face a national campaign by his members. Every farmer in the country would come out in support of the Valley men. Relations with ninety thousand farmers would be destroyed and the minister would have to shoulder the blame. He didn't want another dispute. There had been rows over meat prices, over CAP reform, over compensation for infected stock. A row over the misdemeanours of a few mountainy sheepmen would be a row too far.

Compromise was needed and eventually it was found. The Valley men would have to repay the subsidies they had drawn down for the non existent sheep but there would be no prosecutions. The delegates fought against the repayment of the subsidies but the official side was adamant. The money would have to be repaid. It was European money and the Department had obligations to Brussels. If the books balanced other issues could be swept aside.

"We'll go to the newspapers," one of the delegates told the minister hot headedly.

The minister was alarmed.

"This has got to be kept under cover," he said. "We can't afford to have any publicity. The Department will say nothing to the press but you have to do the same. After all," he went on, " you don't want the good name of the farming community blackened. There would be outcry if the public found out that some of your members had been stealing from the state."

"No one has been stealing anything" the President countered angrily. "A few farmers got out of their depth. They were tempted, but they needed the money to support their families. If the Department hadn't been so lax about enforcing the rules, no one would have got into trouble in the first place."

He sat back triumphantly, satisfied that he had got in a telling blow at the officials.

The minister adopted the mantle of a schoolmaster chastising troublesome students.

"This is a very serious matter," he told the delegation. "People have been caught out in fraud. It can't be tolerated. However, if the money is repaid there will be no further action. But there is to be no publicity. One word to the press and the deal is off."

The delegates went back to farming headquarters, the President satisfied that he had got a good deal. No one would be going to jail. The whole thing would be kept quiet. All the farmers had to do was repay the money.

"It won't be that easy," Tom said as they gathered in one of the committee rooms to discuss the events of the day. "Most of us haven't got the money. Everything we have will have to be sold to pay off the Department. People aren't going to like this. There will be trouble in the Valley."

The President, however, was having none of it. He had negotiated with the Minister, cut a deal for his members and they would have to abide by its terms.

"Just remember that you could all be going to jail," he told Tom angrily. "You've been given a way out. Take it and get on with things."

GREED

Tom drove back to the Valley in a thoughtful frame of mind. He would have to sell what sheep he had as would his neighbours. Even then there wouldn't be enough to cover the refunds.

He went down to the lower farm and told his brother Michael what had happened. They went out to the field and checked the cattle. They weren't exactly in high condition, although the land was marginally better than the home farm.

"What do you think they'll make," Tom asked his brother.

The schoolteacher scratched his chin.

"I doubt if there will be any real profit," he said. "The factories have cut back on the prices again. There's the cost of winter feed. I suppose you'd be better off getting rid of them now and cutting your losses. They might not make any more if you hold them over the winter."

"I'll be wiped out if I have to sell everything off," Tom commented. "It will be hard to start up again."

"You might as well get out of farming altogether" Michael responded. "It's not going to get any better, not for us at any rate. We don't have the land for it. Get out and get a job. You'll be better off."

Tom nodded in agreement. What his brother said made a great deal of sense, but he had the mountain man's reluctance to sell off anything at a loss.

"There's another way," Michael said as they walked back towards the house.

Tom listened intently and agreed that there was indeed another option.

125

Two days later a trailer drew up at the lower farm. Tom was waiting. He went out to meet the driver and paid him what was due and they unloaded a beast and turned it off with the rest of the cattle.

"It will take a few days," The stranger said. "Don't rush things."

He left and Tom leaned over the gate and studied the cattle. The newcomer ranged through them and there was a flurry of activity for a few moments then they all settled down.

Tom smiled grimly to himself. He had found a way out. The Department would get its money but it come from the compensation that he would claim for the loss of his herd. The Department wasn't sharp enough to outwit a Black Valley man. He took a last look at the infected heifer before he drove off home. She was moving amongst the others, spreading the infection that would bring Tom another Department cheque. He would lose his herd from the disease but there would be money in the bank. The Department would pay compensation. It was a farmer's right. The pain and suffering of his cattle were of no consequence. It was all about the money.

Trust

"It's about your son, Paul."

Clodagh stared blankly at the men on her doorstep. One of them pulled out a card.

"We're police officers, from the local station."

For one horrible moment Clodagh thought that they had come to bring her terrible news. Paul had been in an accident, he was killed.

She stared at them, frozen, unable to make any response.

The detective who had spoken to her caught her fear.

"It's alright" he said reassuringly. "It's not what you think. We're here about an assault. Paul's name has been mentioned. We have to ask him some questions."

It was more than questions, the detective could have gone on, but didn't. Paul's name had been mentioned alright. He had been identified as one of the perpetrators of a robbery at corner shop. The owner had been hit with an iron bar. His injuries were serious, but not as they said on the news bulletins, life threatening.

Silently Clodagh brought them into the front room. She had been half expecting this day. Paul was getting more and more out of control, running with a bad crowd, heading for disaster. There had been problems at school when he was younger. He had been expelled twice, had been reported for truancy and fighting. Things had been easier when his father had been around, but just when Clodagh needed him, he had taken off. Clodagh left with two young sons to raise had done her best, but Paul, the eldest, was a lot of trouble.   Peter was easier to manage. He was a pleasant child, got on well at school, and more than compensated for the difficulties which his brother caused.

Clodagh sighed, composed herself and sat down opposite the detectives.

The one who had done all the talking up to now introduced himself.

"Sergeant John O'Hora," he said, and indicated his companion. This is Bill O'Reilly."

Clodagh nodded.

"Is Paul in" O'Reilly asked.

Clodagh shook her head. Paul had gone out at lunchtime and had not returned. The robbery and assault on the shopkeeper had taken place shortly after two o'clock, the detective told her. He asked her where Paul was likely to be. She didn't know. When he went out he often didn't come home until late at night or early in the morning.

"I don't know where he goes," she said. He doesn't tell me anything. In fact he hardly talks to me at all now. He gets his dinner and goes out."

She wiped a tear from the corner of her eye. It had only been a matter of time before Paul got into trouble with the police, but now that it had come, she was unsure of her feelings. Part of her was annoyed that he should bring this to their home, another part of her was defensive, protective, anxious to keep any hint of danger away from him.

The detectives were silent.   This situation was hardly a novel one. They spent most of their time chasing young men for petty crimes. Most of the problems were drink related, but robberies were frequent and drugs a continual headache.

O'Hora raised the drugs issue. Clodagh made no response. She didn't know whether Paul took drugs. If he did they weren't produced at home. But then she saw him so little that he could have been up to anything.

The detective wasn't satisfied. There was no intelligence that Paul Byrne was doing drugs, but they had to ask the question. If he wasn't, he was one of the few. Drugs were a way of life to the young people on the estate. The police had arrested one or two youths for dealing, but by and large it was impossible to stamp the trade out.

 The police were only too well aware that dependency on drugs fuelled crime and seventeen years old Paul Byrne was a criminal. Of this O'Hora was certain. Paul might not yet have a conviction but there had been plenty of incidents in the past where Paul had escaped by a hair's breadth. It was not easy to get evidence and the battle between the police and the recalcitrant youths of the town was never ending. Paul Byrne was one of the most notorious offenders and Sergeant O'Hora was determined that this time there would be no way out for him.

"Can we look in his room," O'Hora asked.

Clodagh was hesitant. She didn't know what rights she had. Paul didn't let anyone into his room. It was his sanctum, a place where he could lose himself and avoid Clodagh's complaints about his manners, his language, his dress, his failure to get enough points to get him into third level education, or his unsuitable friends.

The detectives took her silence for assent and went upstairs.

Clodagh went to the kitchen and put on the kettle. She needed a cup herself and there was also a need to be hospitable even to these unwelcome visitors to her house. The detectives made a thorough search of Paul's bedroom. They were careless in handling Paul's few possessions and it did not take them long to realize that there was nothing there. There was nothing to indicate if Paul was a drug dealer or even a user, no pills, no syringes, and no store of cash which would be hard to explain. They were thorough and kept at it, but eventually had to admit that there was nothing to be found.

They went downstairs again and joined Clodagh in the kitchen. She poured out cups of tea and pushed a packet of biscuits across the table.

"We have got to interview Paul," John O'Hora told his mother. "We have a witness who can identify him as one of the gang that raided his shop. He says that Paul was the one who assaulted him. We'll hold an identification parade to make sure but at the moment it looks as if your son is up to his neck in it. This could mean a jail sentence."

Clodagh was alarmed. The detective made an effort to dispel her concern.

"It's his first offence," he said a note of kindness in his voice. "He might get away with it this time, but he is in very serious trouble."

The other detective, O'Reilly also made an effort to soothe her concerns.

"If he comes clean and owns up, the court might take a lenient view of things. But it all depends on Paul's attitude. If he decides to brazen things out, the judge could decide to send him down."

"You need to talk to your son," John O'Hora said, "and we need to talk to him as well. When he comes home ring us and make an appointment to come down to the station. We'll do the best we can for him."

Clodagh nodded. The tears back in her eyes again. These men were kind but there was a limit to what they could do. She knew that Paul would be unrepentant, belligerent, and totally unco-operative. Youngsters these days despised the police. They had good reason. There was an inherent unfairness in the way they operated. Everyone of them was out to make a name for himself, build up his promotional prospects with convictions. There was no concern, no leeway. The police were out to get them and the young people responded in kind. It was a war, a war in which the teenager tearaways more often than not came out on top.

Evidence was the key to a conviction, and evidence was hard to find, O'Hora thought to himself as they left the house and walked back to their car. The courts were too lenient too concerned with upholding the rights of defendants. The police were given no chance. Miscreants walked free with a slap on the wrist and the police had to explain it all to their victims. The hardest thing to take was the mindless violence that accompanied every raid. Every assault was carried to the extremes. Young fellas as young as fourteen or fifteen were on the prowl, looking out for every opportunity to bring some sort of havoc to other people's lives. Drink and drugs fuelled their activities. Their catalogue of crime was never ending and the police could only do so much.

Sometimes O'Hora felt that he could give it all up. The attraction of the job, the idealism which had driven him as a young police cadet, had long since been dissipated. He was growing old in a daily routine of paltry investigations which led nowhere. Once, and only once, he had been involved in the investigation of a major crime. A man had been murdered and

O'Hora was one of the team assigned to the investigation. It had been wrapped up quickly, too quickly for O'Hora's liking. The murderer had been tracked down expeditiously and had confessed. It was another drink related crime, an argument after closing time, a vicious assault and a session in intensive care for the victim who died after a few days in hospital.

Most of O'Hora's investigations were centred on robberies and street violence. The robberies invariably followed the same pattern. A couple of youths would enter a premises, threaten or assault the owner and take off with the takings of the day. This was the case with the robbery in which Paul was implicated, except on this occasion the assault had been more than unusually vicious. The shopkeeper was from the locality and had recognized Paul as his assailant. As a case it was open and shut. If the shopkeeper confirmed his identification Paul would go down.

O'Hora's thoughts wandered back to the boy's mother. She was an attractive women, a bit worn from the difficulties which she had faced in bringing up two children alone, but she had kept her looks. O'Hora too had a broken marriage. His wife had left him five years ago. It had been an amicable arrangement. They had grown apart and were prepared to admit it. Since then there were casual affairs but nothing long term. O'Hora was ready for something more permanent. He had an eye for a pretty woman, and Clodagh in her early forties had held her looks and her figure. She was, O'Hora decided, a tasty piece. It was a pity about the son though. But then he thought, the boy's problems might prove to be a way of drawing them together.

Acting on an impulse he went back to Clodagh's house. Paul still hadn't returned home, but she invited him in. Both of them settled down in front of the television which was a distraction for O'Hora as he wanted to talk. The woman sensing his impatience switched it off and they started a conversation. The detective drew her out about herself, the break-up of her marriage and her problems with the two boys. Peter, her second son, was four years younger than Paul. He was in the kitchen doing his homework.

He was no trouble, Clodagh told the policeman. The exact opposite of Paul. The younger boy had settled well into school from the start, did his homework every night and showed no disposition towards emulating the never ending trail of trouble that was Paul's life. The detective sympathized with her when she talked about Paul and gave acquiescent nods and expressions of approval when she contrasted him with his younger brother. O'Hora was pleased with the progress he was making. Even though their association had so far lasted no more than a few hours there was a rapport. The woman liked him, he was certain.

For her part Clodagh sensed that she was addressing a man who was understanding and sympathetic. The fact that he was a policeman did not automatically exclude these values, she felt. She was still conscious, however, that Paul was his quarry. He wouldn't be sitting in her house having this conversation if it had not been for the fact that her elder son was in trouble, serious trouble according to the detective earlier that day.

The evening wore on. The detective was comfortable, relaxed, enjoying the experience. It was not often that he spent an evening with an attractive woman. When his shift was finished he usually went to the pub for an hour or two and then went home calling into a fast food shop for something to eat on the way. He knew that he should get up and go. The last thing he wanted was to outstay his welcome. If Paul came back he would have to arrest him and this would create a rift in this burgeoning relationship with his mother. Finally he decided that he had been there long enough. He got up. The woman followed him to the front door.

"Don't worry too much about Paul," he said. "I'll have a talk with him tomorrow. Things might not be as bad as they look."

Inside he knew that the reality was that Paul was in serious trouble. The shopkeeper had been viciously assaulted, and there had been damage to the shop and stock as well. The detective wondered whether he could persuade the shopkeeper to back off and then dismissed the thought. He was allowing his feelings for the boy's mother to cloud his better judgment. There was no way that he could interfere with the course of events. There was no question of suppressing the case. The boy was in trouble and he would have to make the best of things. If jail was the end result of the case then so be it. Paul and his mother would have to live with it.

O'Hora knew that Clodagh would be distraught if Paul was convicted and sent away. That she loved her wayward son was without question. That she would have to cope with events as they came along was also a given. However, O'Hora thought that he might stay in her life as a counsellor and comforter. The woman was worth pursuing, but he had to make sure that he wasn't compromised in any way. A personal association with the mother of a boy whom he was investigating would not be countenanced by his superiors. The Superintendent was a stickler for discipline and would come down heavily on anyone who got out of line.

John O'Hora's ambition from the days when he left school had been to be a detective. He had passed the cadet course at the training college with honours and after seven years handed in his uniform join the plain clothes branch. Later he had taken the sergeant's examination, and seemed set on the promotional ladder. However, further advancement had eluded him. He didn't get the high profile cases and eventually disinterest and inertia had settled in. He had no ambition now to become an inspector. He went through the motions of the daily round of trivial investigations and allowed opportunities to attract the attention of his superiors to drift by.

The breakup of his marriage had finally eradicated all thoughts of further advancement. He was content with his lot. Occasionally there was a burst of the old enthusiasm if a particular case created challenges, but for the most part his stimulation came from the occasional pursuit of a particularly nasty piece of work. He got a vicarious satisfaction if he succeeded in sending someone to jail. Administering the vengeance of the law compensated for his personal failures. if they escaped with a minor rebuke from the bench he accepted it philosophically. It was the way things were. The ultimate goal was a good result. Once a detective, always a detective. No one could be allowed to get away. A detective was always on duty.

The Paul Byrne case had a special piquancy. There was the fact that a particularly vicious assault had taken place, a crime which would satisfy the detective's predatory instincts if it came to the expected conclusion. But there was the added dimension that the boy's mother was an attractive woman. O'Hora could sense the fact that he had an advantage. The woman was vulnerable. The detective could play the role of a sympathetic well wisher to perfection. On most occasions his talents were directed at getting a result, eliciting information that would lead to a courtroom appearance by his subject. This time there was another dimension. He was interested in Clodagh Byrne. It was a purely sexual attraction. She was desirable. Her son was in trouble. O'Hora was keen. There would at some stage be some degree of fusion.

He went back to the Byrne house the following day, deliberately assigning his partner to another investigation so that he would be able to make his visit alone. Paul Byrne was in this time. His mother called him downstairs and the three of them sat together in the kitchen. Clodagh made cups of coffee. The detective got straight to the point.

135

"You're in trouble, Paul," he said. "We know you robbed the shop and hit the old man. Your best chance now is to admit it and I will try and convince the court that you were helpful and should be looked on favourably."

The youth said nothing, but his expression gave away his inward feelings. He was sullen, belligerent, all the emotions which his mother knew so well were in charge.

O'Hora ignored this. He was well used to antagonism from the young hoodlums he encountered every day.

"For your mother's sake," he went on suavely. "Give up on this. It will be the better for you in the long run. I'll take you down to the station and you can make a statement. You'll get immediate bail. I'll see to that."

Clodagh intervened.

"Do what Mr O'Hora asks, Paul," she said pleadingly. "It's for the best."

Tears came and there was an uncomfortable silence in the room for a few minutes.

O'Hora leaned across the table and took the woman's hands in his.

"Don't worry," he said. "We'll make the best of this."

He turned to Paul again adopting a sterner tone.

"Look what you're doing to your mother," he said. "You've upset her. Don't make things any worse than they are."

The boy wouldn't give in. He stared silently into one corner of

136

the room. O'Hora sighed. This was going to be difficult. If the youth continued to adopt this stance very little progress could be made.

O'Hora was annoyed. He had tried to meet the boy halfway, but he had got nowhere. He turned to the mother.

"Perhaps you could give us a few minutes alone."

She got up and left the room. They could hear her footsteps upstairs as she busied herself with some domestic chores.

O'Hora got up went around the table and took the boy by the shoulder.

"Listen to me, you little rat," he said viciously. "Either you make a statement or I'll see that you go away for a long time. The old man is in hospital. You put him there. Unless you co-operate the courts will give you the maximum sentence. And it won't be in any young offenders prison either. You'll be locked up with the big boys, drugs dealers, murders, the scum of the earth. You won't have a comfortable place to come home to in the evenings. You won't have your mother to cook and keep house for you. You'll be locked up three to a cell and you'll stay there for years."

The boy was frightened. The detective's onslaught had taken him by surprise. He got up and faced O'Hora. He still wasn't prepared to give in.

"I did nothing," he said defiantly. "You'll have to prove it was me. I'm saying nothing to you or anyone else."

With that he ran out of the room and the front door slammed. He was gone.

Clodagh came down the stairs and joined the detective in the

kitchen. She was tense, white faced. O'Hora put the kettle on
again and made some tea. She accepted a cup in silence and
sat down miserably at the table.

"You'll have to get to work on him," he said after a moment
or two. "I don't want him to be a fugitive. There are no
charges as yet. We're still investigating, but I'll have to take
some sort of action very soon. The Super will be on my back
for a result. It was a serious offence. They won't let it go."

She nodded her understanding of the situation and wiped her
eyes. He leaned across the table and took bother her hands in
his own.

"I'll do anything I can to help," he promised. "Anything, but
the boy has to co-operate."

She understood. She allowed her hands to remain in his clasp
for a few more minutes and then took them away. O'Hora
sensed that he had won her over. This was a woman who faced
adversity but somehow had found a champion in the very man
who was bringing trouble to her door.

He stayed for over an hour. Paul didn't come back but she
promised that she would talk to him when he did.

"Remember that I'm your friend," the detective said as they
stood for a few more moments at the front door. "I'll help. I
promise you that."

He went off into the night, his spirits lifted by the thought that
he was on the verge of establishing a relationship with
Clodagh Byrne. The son's escapade had brought them
together. Things could only get better. He was ready for a
relationship. It had been a couple of years since he had felt
anything for a woman and the prospect of a new fresh liaison
was more than tempting.

TRUST

He wondered what he should do about the boy. His promises to his mother were all very well, but O'Hara knew that there was very little that he could do for Paul. O'Hora was a policeman first and foremost and applied himself vigilantly to every investigation. He was a man permanently in pursuit of a quarry, and Paul Byrne was a serious quarry. His superiors would expect a result and quickly, once they realised that the perpetrator had been identified. The best that he could do was to stall things for a while, and give Paul an opportunity to make things right. That meant an admission, and the clear prospect of a jail sentence, but the sentence would be reduced if he confessed.

O'Hora knew that he had promised Clodagh much more than this. He could see no way out of the situation. His duty was clear. There could be no compromise. Clodagh would be devastated, but there was an upside from the detective's perspective. With the boy out of the way, he would have a clear run at his mother. She would need a man's shoulder. The detective could live with the fact that she was a criminal's mother. Long associations with crime had imbued a tolerance of both the people and the events in which they were emeshed. Criminals were there to be hunted down with a ruthless perseverance that compensated for the fact that O'Hora had no other interests in his life. Their distracted families and friends were unfortunates who attracted little sympathy. They were sources and leads to getting the result which O'Hora was duty bound to provide.

This time it was different. Clodagh Byrne was a temptation. She could lead him astray. He was only sorry that her son had got himself into so serious a difficulty. If there had been a lesser offence he could have done more for her, but as it was he could only masquerade at relieving her of her pain.

He called again the following morning. Clodagh had stayed up half the night until Paul had eventually come in. They had talked for several hours, she told the detective. Paul would make a statement, relying on O'Hora to do the best he could for him

O'Hora warmed to the woman and cemented their friendship with an assurance that he would stand by Paul. He brought the boy to the station. They had a short session in an interview room and Paul signed a statement confessing to the assault and the robbery of the store. O'Hora smiled grimly as he picked up the couple of sheets of paper that Paul had used to write out his confession. Then came the formalities of arrest and charge. It was only when they put him into a cell that Paul realized that he was trapped. He would be in court the following morning, O'Hora told him. The police would be opposing bail.

O'Hora went out to his desk and completed the paper work. He was bringing it out to the front office when he met the Superintendent in the corridor.

"A good result," the Superintendent commented. "Up to your usual standards, a good clean cut case. The boy will go down and deserves it all."

O'Hora smiled briefly at the words of praise from his senior officer. He had done his job, got the result that was required. Once a policeman, always a policeman. Other considerations did not apply. The goal was the result, the conviction, and the subsequent satisfaction of knowing that no one had got away. Tomorrow he would have to face Clodagh Byrne. He could live with that. A policeman was always on duty.

Anger

They sat together in the pub, in their favourite corner. They had been there many times before but this time it was different.

Miriam chose her words carefully. She had made her decision. Now she had to impart it to her boyfriend. There was no going back. It had to end. But even though her mind was made up it was difficult to put her feelings into words. Adrian would take it badly, She knew that. He would get angry, storm at her, throw down his glass and probably run out of the pub into the night. Then he would be back, hammering at her front door, demanding to be admitted. Roaring and cursing. She had gone through this before, a decision made, only to be undone in the face of Adrian's outbursts.

This time it was going to be different. Her mind was made up. She didn't love him. All that was over months ago. She couldn't face his mood swings, his jealousy, his possessiveness, any longer. This time they were going to split. It was final. There would be no going back.

She had told her parents of her decision at breakfast that morning. They were relieved. Their daughter's relationship with Adrian Crowley had been worrying them for some time now. She was clearly unhappy and they wanted it to end. They knew better than to interfere, of course, but this announcement and the tone of finality in their daughter's voice had been more than welcome. There were other young men in the locality any of whom would be more than willing to step into Adrian's place.

"It's over, Adrian" she told him. "I want to break up, for good this time. I need to get to know other people, to be free again. We've been together too long. It isn't doing either of us any good. This is the last time we'll be together."

She waited for an onslaught but to her surprise Adrian was quiet. She glanced at him quickly and was shocked. Tears were coursing down his cheeks. He sat there in silence, allowing his misery to ease its way out. He didn't sob. Just sat there, crying silently. She didn't know what to do. This wasn't the reaction she had expected. Shouting yes, some name calling and cursing, but this flood of silent misery was different, strange, alarming even.

There was nothing more she could say. She got up and left the pub, walking home alone, disturbed by the reaction she had provoked. For some time now she had wondered about Adrian's moods. When they first started going out together he was carefree, considerate, always cheerful, always good for a laugh. Their early relationship had been casual, undemanding, a couple of evenings out together during the week, week-end trips to concerts in Dublin, all the usual activities which young people undertook in the course of their coming together. Slowly, imperceptibly, he had changed, becoming more morose, difficult, their evenings punctuated by angry outbursts followed by intense apologies and fevered reconciliations.

They had discussed moving in together but Miriam had sidestepped this. She was gradually becoming more and more concerned about Adrian and was less and less inclined to see him as a long term prospect. On his good days, he was cheerful, companionable, but when the dark clouds descended, he became insufferable, and she was glad to get away from him. There was no one else on the horizon. They had been together for nearly two years, and their friends accepted them as an item, with anyone else who might have been interested getting the message that they were a pair who were not for parting. Now the parting had finally come. But Miriam wasn't really easy in her mind. It had been too easy. Adrian's flood of tears had disturbed her. It wasn't like him, but perhaps he too had realized that it was all over and that his misery was the precursor of a more balanced approach to the situation.

ANGER

Adrian was a farmer's son, he had completed his time at Gurteen College and had his certificate. Miriam's father was an accountant and worked at one of the American owned factories on the edge of the town. Miriam was waiting to go to college and had a part time job. Both of them were free in the evenings and Adrian usually managed to pick her up around eight o'clock. At first Miriam's parents were pleased that she had made out with a pleasant and apparently quiet country boy. Then over time the difficulties had arisen. Miriam confided in her mother to some extent but mostly she kept her problems to herself. Finally when things had got too much out of hand they gave her some direct advice.

"Get rid of him," her father had said. "He's obviously difficult and you don't want to have him around any longer. He's trouble. You have your degree to think about. Concentrate on that and forget him."

Getting rid of Adrian was more easily said than done, but now it had finally happened. She had steeled herself to make the decision, to finally confront him and put an end to a relationship which was becoming more and more troubled with every passing day.

Her parents were waiting for her in the television room. She told them briefly what had transpired, omitting any mention of Adrian's breakdown and went to bed. She should have been easy in her mind, but she was strangely troubled, found it hard to get to sleep and got up the next morning with circles under her eyes. The rest of the evening passed without any sign of Adrian. Evidently he had taken her decision to heart. She was relieved. Gradually the expectancy that Adrian would be back, pleading, demanding, intent on resuming their association, passed. She felt that it was over, that he had accepted the situation and that life could go on in a more measured way. Her relationship with Adrian was an experience that she wanted to forget, and his apparent acquiescence made

143

forgetting that much easier.

Adrian left the pub in a daze. He had stayed there for at least half an hour after Miriam's departure. He stopped crying after around five minutes and ignoring the curious glances of those around him, miserably contemplated life without his girl friend. She had threatened to break up on several previous occasions but each time Adrian had managed to turn her around. This time, he knew, she meant it. There was a void inside him, an emptiness which he could not drive away. Not that he had any real inclination to brace himself after Miriam's departure. He was content to lapse into his misery, to take a perverse kind of comfort in a belief that he was a victim, a person cruelly wronged by his girlfriend who had thrown away all the good and close times that they had together.

In this frame of mind he eventually pushed his way out of the pub and wandered aimlessly along the road towards his home. Normally he would have got a taxi, but tonight he had no interest in getting home. The night offered him some balm for his misery, he could think things through, he could come to decisions. He was determined that this was not going to be the end of the matter. Irrespective of Miriam's determination he would push for a reconciliation. These were his first thoughts, as he walked on his feelings gradually turned to anger. The bitch, why had she done this to him. She was ungrateful, selfish, gratuitously throwing away the opportunity of a life together.

That Miriam might have had just cause to break things off never entered his head. He neither considered nor cared that he was difficult, sullen, or given to threats of violence. He had never laid hands on her, never even pushed her, despite the fact that he had often been so angry. He had a temper, he knew, but his actions had always been governed by the realization that if he allowed himself to engage in violence he would lose her forever.

144

ANGER

Now he had lost her anyway. He had nothing to reproach himself with. It was all down to Miriam. She was the aggressor. She had used him shamelessly and when she wanted to take up with other people had cast him aside. The fact that there had never been any suggestion that Miriam had anyone else in mind was irrelevant. He had seen the way she looked at other young men. She was shameless, a slut. She had not deserved his loyalty.

He walked on, furious now, hammering one clenched fist into a palm in an expression of his turmoil. Then his anger suddenly dissipated and he began to feel sorry for himself. He started to cry again but still walked on towards home, ignoring the tears that ran down his cheeks. There was no one to see in the dark and he could let himself go without any thought of being overlooked.

After awhile the rage came back. He quickened his pace in the urgency of his paroxysm, marching now at a rate which was only a few steps short of running. His fury increased with the rapidity of his footsteps, and he began to curse out loud, shouting into the night breeze, the raucous disturbing sounds drifting away into the darkness. He passed one or two houses along the roadside and quietened until he had left the lights from their windows behind. Then he began to shout again. Suddenly he was tired and he sat down at the side of the road, ignoring an occasional passing car. No one stopped. The drivers probably didn't even see him in the dark. He didn't care. He wanted to be alone. Misery was a luxury best sampled in solitude.

He lay back against the ditch and closed his eyes. Tiredness swam in and he drifted off into a few moments of fitful uncomfortable sleep. A light drizzle of rain started to fall but he ignored it. The cold of the autumn evening made no impression on him either. The awful blow of his loss overwhelmed him. Miriam had broken up their lives, had

145

thrown everything away. How could she do this. They were part of each other. He was grieving just as if he had suffered a bereavement, lost someone in his family. He had lost someone. Miriam was the most precious thing in his life. He lay in the dampness of the night and allowed a cloud of pain to envelop him. After awhile, the cold and the damp penetrated his body and he got up and resumed walking. The rhythm of his movements encouraged a new train of thought in his mind. If he couldn't have her then no one would. He could end it all, they could go out together. Miriam would suffer for her ingratitude, her ruthless determination to sunder their relationship, but in the end she would be grateful to him. They would be together, locked in a final embrace which no one could disturb.

A decision made, Adrian walked rapidly homewards. He didn't go to bed but spent the rest of the night huddled in an armchair in the sitting room. His head was pounding, a steady rhythm of hammer blows that seemed to accompany every breath. He slept fitfully, waking every half hour or so, conscious of the need to rapidly reach daylight. This would be a momentous day. He would accomplish his destiny, his and Miriam's. She would be grateful to him, secure in the knowledge that they were together, never to be parted. He fell into a longer sleep in the early hours and woke up as his mother came downstairs to prepare the breakfast.

She was surprised to see him there, concerned, taking in his white face, his disheveled clothes, all the evidence that her son had passed a tumultuous night. She asked him solicitously if he would like a cup of tea, but he ignored her, rushed upstairs to the bathroom and splashed his face with water. Unrefreshed but eager to get on with the momentous task he had set himself he went to the gun safe. It was locked but he knew where the key was kept. He grabbed a single barreled shotgun and half a dozen cartridges and rushed out into the yard. His brother's car was there and within seconds he was in the

146

driving seat and heading for the town.

A mile short of Miriam's house he pulled up and parked. He got out of the car and paced the roadway. The shotgun lay on the front passenger seat, a challenge to his decision to end it all. The pounding in his head increased but despite his conviction that there was only one way to go, a flood of indecision engulfed him. What he contemplated was a terrible act. A crime, a deed which would damn his soul for all eternity. Memories of his childhood church going days crowded his mind, the guilt, the sins which had seemed so terrible at the time, the rehearsed recitals to the priest in confession, the penances that now seemed so paltry. How could he get absolution for murder and self destruction.

His head ached with the constant pounding in his brain and he got back into the car and lay against the headrest. He began to cry, a bitter sobbing that evoked all the misery that he felt. Indecision reigned. Perhaps there was another way out. Perhaps Miriam could be persuaded to change her mind. Eagerly he grasped at the thought, converting the wish into fact. Yes, this was the way to go. To appeal to Miriam once more, to make her see that their love was never ending. They could be together. Everything would be back the way it used to be.

The pounding in his head eased with the relief of finding another way out. He lay there for half an hour or more, then refreshed with the relief that he was not going to go through with the terrible act, started the car again and drove on. The early sun caught the windscreen and he found it hard to see ahead. He slowed down, anxious to ensure that he didn't drive into oncoming cars. An accident now would destroy his idyll. Nothing must be allowed to come between himself and Miriam, nothing must sunder the reunion that was about to take place.

147

He stopped again, this time only a short distance from Miriam's gate. He began to rehearse what he would say. He would remind her of the good times, of the moments of tenderness and commitment, of their promises to stay together. He closed his eyes and allowed his thoughts to wander over the months of their relationship. They had done many things, gone to many places, concert, festivals, discos. They had exchanged many presents. He had bought her a gold necklace and she had responded with an expensive watch. They had lain out under the stars and basked on sandy beaches along the coast in the summer time. There had been long walks in the mountains and excursions to Dublin, long week-ends in Ballybunion, and one day trips to Sligo and the Yeats country. Yes, he would remind her of all these things. He was certain that she did not really mean to break them up. It was a form of teasing, an attempt to hurt him a little so that there would be a reunion and a renewal of the passion that they forged between them.

The pounding in his head came back again. Rage once more consumed him. How dare she treat him like this. He didn't deserve to be put through all this pain. He hadn't looked at another girl since they began to treat their relationship in a serious way. But could the same be said of her. His mind flashed over the other young men that she knew. Was there a feeling for one, concern for another. Was her demand for freedom founded on admiration for another man. Had she secretly been seeing someone behind his back. He converted these thoughts into fact. She had been unfaithful, he told himself. She had gone with someone else. Another man was poised to step into his place. That was why she wanted to break up. His anger was unabated. He took up the gun and levered in a cartridge. Then he stepped out along the road, the gun under his arm, black prejudice and anger suffocating all sense of reason.

Miriam saw him from her bedroom window. He was standing

148

on the front lawn, his shirt open to the waist, the gun under his arm. She stared at him for several minutes. He stood motionless, white faced, apparently totally unaware of his surroundings. She wasn't concerned about the gun. He often went shooting and she had been out with him a few times, stalking the hedgerows for a stray rabbit or perhaps even a pheasant. They bred in the locality, the descendants of birds which had escaped from one of the larger local estates.

She was about to open the window and speak to him when her father came around the side of the house. He walked across the lawn to Adrian and put his hand out to take the gun. Adrian drew away, but made no attempt to raise the weapon. Her father talked with him for a few minutes and then abruptly left and came back into the house.

He called up to her bedroom.

"Miriam, come down and talk to Adrian. He seems to be upset. He has no business being here at this hour of the morning. We haven't even had breakfast yet. Get rid of him. Tell him to go away. He won't listen to me."

Miriam sighed. The last thing she needed at the start of the day was a repetition of the previous evening's outbursts. Why couldn't he accept things for what they were. She had spoken out plainly. Their romance was over. She definitely didn't want to go on. He was so immature. That was one of the reasons she had broken off with him. That he wanted her was plain enough, but she didn't want him. She had had enough of her association with an overgrown child.

She ran down the stairs and went out through the front door. He made no move in her direction. Just stood their silently, ashen faced, the gun under his arm.

She wasn't concerned. He was familiar with guns and she had

149

learned to accept them, although the noise of the shot and the impact in a rabbit's soft body or the dismembering of a bird repulsed her. She had put up with it because shooting was something he apparently liked to do. It had brought them out into the countryside together, and had been a form of bonding.

"Adrian. You can't come here like this. My father is annoyed. Go home. We're finished together. You'll have to accept that."

He made no response. Just stood there staring blankly into space.

She made another attempt to get through to him, annoyed herself this time.

"Adrian. Go home. You can't come here like this. Go home."

Again he ignored her.

She reached out to him and caught his arm. For the first time he seemed to be aware of her presence. But still he said nothing.

Irritated she shook him, attempting to break him out of his lethargy. The last thing she expected was that he would harm her. He had a temper, yes, and she had encountered it often enough, but he had never struck her. The gun was just something he was carrying. She shook him again and he focused on her face.

"You've destroyed me," he said brokenly. "Look what you've made me do."

With that he raised the gun and fired point blank into her chest. She felt the pain for a fleeting second then crumpled to the ground.

150

ANGER

Miriam's father came rushing out of the house. He stood for a few horrified moments looking at his daughter's body on the ground. Blood was spreading slowly through her blouse and out on to the lawn.

Adrian fumbled in his pocket for another cartridge and for one terrible moment Bill Maxwell's horror at what had happened to his daughter was supplanted by fear for himself.

He stared transfixed at Adrian expecting the worst, not that there could be anything worse than finding the lifeless body of his daughter lying there, the victim of this deranged young man who had once professed himself so much in love.

For his part Adrian stared unseeingly at his erstwhile lover's father. A cold fear grasped him. He had done a terrible thing. But his resolve was unshaken. The two of them would leave together. He took a last look at Miriam's body then raised the gun, put the barrel in his mouth and pulled the trigger.

The sound of the second shot brought Miriam's mother out into the garden. She began to scream. Her husband gathered his daughter in his arms and sobbed, harsh dry racking sobs. The desolation of Miriam's parents was total, overwhelming, never to be put aside.

Adrian's parents wanted a joint funeral. They came the following night to the Maxwell house. Bill Maxwell met them at the door, tight lipped, bitter.

"There is no question of anything like that," he said. "It would be an insult to my daughter's memory to lay them down together.

Adrian's father, broken, bowed put out his hand to Bill Maxwell.

"We're grieving too," he said. "We've lost our son. We should share our grief together" he said in strangled tones. Maxwell thrust the outstretched hand away.

"We want nothing to do with your family," he said. "Your son murdered our beautiful daughter. We cannot forgive you or your son. We're glad he's dead. Go away and don't come back here again. We are desolate people. Your son destroyed our happiness. We don't care about your grief. We have our own."

He wanted to hit back but there was no target. Adrian was dead and these pathetic supplicating parents were no substitute. He had to suppress his anger, but it was there inside him and would be there for the rest of his life.

Adrian Crowley too had been angry, tormented. But it had been a different kind of anger, fuelled by the passions to which he had been subjected and the stricken state of his mind. The anger of Miriam's father was forged from different circumstances. It was the anger borne of overwhelming grief and there was no solution, no cure. His distress would be with him all his days, a dreadful burden of unremitting pain.

Success

Everyone agreed. Matt Dillon was the brains of the family. Even when he was going to school, he was streets ahead of his older brother Joey. The Dillon boys were marked down as tearaways, always in trouble, mitching, vandalising, drinking, but it was always Joey who was hammered. He was the eldest. He should be giving his younger brother good example. Those closest to the family, however, knew that it was Matt who was making the running. Sharp, quick witted, whatever terms you used to describe him, they always paid tribute to his domineering qualities and his ability to get away with as much as possible.

But Matt had other attributes. He was a juvenile entrepreneur, always alert to the opportunity of making a profit on something, buying cheap and sell on a margin, wheeling and dealing in unlikely commodities that met the laws of supply and demand. Although still in primary school he demonstrated a flair for trade and commerce that marked him out for a prosperous future. But there was a reckless streak there too, and there were those who predicted that one day he would press his luck too far.

Joey was used to taking the blame. His brother led and he followed. There were times when he baulked at some particular piece of mischief but mostly he did as Matt commanded. Reveling in the thrill of it all and reconciled to the fact that eventually he would be the one who would have to pay the penalty while Matt invariably got away with it. But the strictures of teachers and police were nothing compared to the excitement of being Matt's right hand man.

Their mother Kathleen was a single parent. When neighbours criticized her sons and indeed herself for permitting them to run wild, she used her status as a shield and an excuse.

"They're boys," she would say defensively. "They're high spirited. I would sooner have them that way than cowed and timid."

The neighbours gave up and went about their lives hoping that the depredations of the Dillon boys would not impinge too much on their daily affairs.

Matt was smart at school. Despite the fact that there were many days lost which were spent larking around the mall or in the amusement arcade, he could master everything the teachers could throw at him. He made no apparent effort but he always emerged at around the top of the class. Joey was plodding, suffered from his missed days at school, and more often than not languished near the bottom.

Matt was earmarked for third level education. Joey would have to take his chances in the jobs market when he left secondary school. Kathleen revelled in Matt's good results and felt for Joey who clearly would have a much more difficult time in making his way in the world. Matt would surely land a good job in electronics or business. Joey would have to be content with stints as a builders' labourer or a shop assistant.

This was in the future. In the meantime Kathleen had to cope with complaints and visits from the police who issued dire warnings that her boys were in with a bad crowd and sooner or later would get into serious trouble. Kathleen counselled her sons without much confidence in the outcome. They made up their own minds about their activities, Joey inclined to be compliant, Matt headstrong and contemptuous of warnings from any source, not just the police.

Their schooldays over, Matt and Joey embarked on separate highways. Matt worked for a year or two in several jobs but couldn't settle down to any particular career. Joey got a job as a shop assistant and was content to draw down a weekly wage packet. Matt had other ideas. He exploited his knack for wheeling and dealing, focused on building a successful and profitable career. By the time he was twenty three he owned a half share in a pub. Three years later he was the sole owner. His business partner complained bitterly that he had been shafted, that Matt had used the business's own earnings to buy him out, but Matt ignored these protestations. He sold the pub at a profit and reinvested in a small hotel. This didn't fare as well and he got out at loss. Joey meantime continued at his humdrum job, drew down his wages and was content.

Matt bought into a furniture business, stuck with it for the best part of a year and got out. The business was profitable enough, but it was tame. Matt thrived on excitement. He needed a challenge. Risk was second nature to him and ordinary run of the mill activities, slow building safe successes were of no interest. He wanted to be rich, to be powerful, and he realized that he would have to get into areas where risk was second nature but the rewards were spectacular.

It was inevitable that he would turn to more exotic activities to satisfy his ambition. The drugs business offered huge opportunities and the commensurate amount of risk. Matt at first proceeded cautiously. He wasn't into retail dealing, the sale of a few tablets to adolescent youths looking for kicks. He was determined to get into the wholesale end, to import in large quantities and pass on his product to eager gangland figures who like himself realized that the real money was in the lethal drugs, heroin, crack cocaine, bought and sold in bulk.

Matt got to know figures in the drugs trade, but was careful not to let himself be too closely identified with them. He knew that it would be easy to attract the attention of the authorities, and that this time there would not be cautionary visits from fatherly community policemen dispensing friendly advice. The Drug Squad detectives were determined men, engaged in a fight to keep evil and destruction off the streets. The level at which Matt was keen to enter the trade was high cost, high risk and could see him languishing in jail for ten to twelve years or more if things went wrong.

He went to Holland to seek out suppliers for himself and cautiously got to know the people there. They were tough hard men, callous in the extreme about the anguish that their product brought to so many people. They were interested in profit and Matt could understand that. It was what he himself was about. There was money to be made in the drugs trade if you got in big enough. Matt had some money put by but not enough. He needed to raise extra cash to buy the benefits that drug running would bring.

Matt thought things over. His proceeds from his previous investments were available but he needed greater capital. His business sense and experience to date had taught him that there were sources of ready money. Banks were prime targets. He had a good record and they would surely listen if he put up a plan for a new business. It would be a scam of course. The bank would advance capital for one business but Matt would divert it into the drugs trade, with a far greater level of profit. He could pay back the bank, keep his good financial record, and have a small fortune as a result. The more Matt thought about his plan, the more he believed he could carry it off.

Banks were gullible. They were in business to lend money to entrepreneurs. Matt was an entrepreneur but his ambitions lay in a darker direction. Not for him the daily round of minute attention to legitimate trading, the commitment to quality, to public relations. Matt was interested in more exciting things. The thrill of outwitting the authorities, the lure of vast profits, and the exciting lifestyle that a rich man could lead. Visions of the future swam before his eyes, fast cars, yachts, exotic women, a luxurious lifestyle. Matt knew that it could not be accomplished in the normal way. It would take years of plodding in a small town business to yield even a fraction of what was in his sights.

Matt applied all his talents to his new trade. He raised cash from the bank, added it to his own nest egg and invested in his first consignment of heroin. He brought it into the country in a specially converted truck and because he was new and unknown to the authorities got away with it. Other trips to Holland followed and he made other connections at home. He became known in the trade as a reliable source and there were plenty of eager takers for what he had to offer. His profits piled up but always there was the thirst for more. Soon his own single trips to the Continent did not yield enough product, produce enough of a return. He expanded, employing couriers, but always taking care to manage the handovers secretly and effectively so that there would be no leaks to the police, reducing the chances of getting caught.

His contemporaries in the business believed that Matt was a kingpin. Certainly he seemed to lead a charmed life. Other dealers were getting caught, the Drug Squad regularly seized huge hauls of illicit contraband, and many of the gangs lost heavily. But Matt's consignments kept getting through. He was boastful.

"It takes brains to succeed in this business," he boasted. "I can stay ahead of the best of them. They'll never catch me."

And so it seemed. Matt amassed more and more money, paid off his debt to the bank and invested in other businesses. These too yielded their share of profit, but Matt's richest source of income was from the drugs trade and he continued to operate side by side with his legitimate enterprises.

He took Joey out of his mediocre job and made him a manager in one of the chain of pubs that he had bought. Joey was

157

compliant, appreciating the extra money and the fact that his brother had looked out for him. Kathleen was content, satisfied that she had done the best for her sons and that they had prospered accordingly. Matt wanted to buy her a new house but she turned him down. She wanted to stay where she was with the neighbours she knew. She accepted some new furniture and a couple of holidays abroad, but that was the limit to her demands on her prosperous son.

She knew nothing of his investment in drugs, believed that his success flowed from natural flair and ability. As she grew older, Kathleen took comfort in the belief that she had brought up a son who would take care of her in her declining years. She didn't expect much of Joey. It was Matt who was her star.

Matt's affluence brought other advantages. He was as successful with women as he had been in business and there were plenty of brief liaisons with both single and married women. One affair nearly ended in disaster. An outraged husband sought him out and Matt had to suffer the indignity of a very public physical assault. He got his revenge. Two nights later a couple of thugs paid the angry husband a visit. Still it was a lesson for Matt. He was more careful in future, concentrating on glamorous unattached women who came without strings and could be discarded at will.

But Matt was a flattering and rewarding Romeo. Every woman thrust aside had been showered with gifts and in time he applied the same skills to parting as he had given to business. Matt's career as a lothario was as brilliant as his rise to power and plenty. Rumours abounded and they soon came to the attention of the Drugs Squad. But there was no hard evidence and the stern upholders of the law were unable to move against him. But they promised themselves there would be another day. Matt would make a mistake and they would be ready to pounce.

SUCCESS

Eventually Matt found a woman with whom he wanted to settle down. He courted and won her. It was a lavish wedding. Hundreds of guests attended, the presents were glittering and expensive. Sheelagh was tall, attractive, came from a good family background and was very much in love. For a time Matt concentrated solely on her, and cut back on his illegal operations. He applied himself to his legitimate businesses, no longer wanting to risk anything that might mar his happiness. But eventually the brightness of married life, the novelty of true love began to pall. Relations with Sheelagh became perfunctory, casual. He renewed his associations with other women and the lure of the drugs trade loomed strong again. It wasn't just the money. There was a thrill to the business. The profits were huge, of course, but Matt knew that he was running close to the wind, that he was assuming great risks. The scent of danger stirred his adrenalin, he was driven by the risks, and his unbounded confidence in himself. They couldn't catch him. He had the brains, the skills which allowed him to outwit the lesser men who pursued him.

Joey was pleased with his role in life. His brother's rise to the status of a tycoon had thrilled and stimulated him. Matt had been bountiful in his success. He had been good to their mother and had conferred new status on Joey himself. Joey appreciated his role as pub manager, the good wages which the job paid, but there was a downside. From time to time Matt called upon him to carry out missions which ran close to the wind and Joey realized that the dark forces which drove his brother could at any time engulf him also. Matt was careful about himself, he took precautions, but Joey like any one else in his organization was expendable. Joey was under no illusions. There was a hard streak to Matt. If things went wrong Joey would be left to suffer just as he had been made the scapegoat for depredations when they were children.

As Matt resumed his underworld trading rumours began to circulate again. The stern men in the Drug Squad pricked up

159

their ears and Matt became a target. Men and resources were piled on the trail and every move was noted, every contact assessed, every casual detail of his life overhauled and researched.

It was Joey who realised that there was trouble ahead. He picked up casual conversations in the bar, noted how the detectives concentrated on every aspect of their lives. But Matt took no heed. He was convinced that he was impregnable, that no one could bring him down. He was too clever, too ruthless, too resourceful. He had powerful friends, he controlled a vast empire of business legal and illegal, and he had the money too see off every challenger.

But the endgame arrived, as Joey had forewarned. Matt made a mistake. He allowed a link with himself to be exposed. One of his minions turned and provided the evidence that the detectives needed and Matt was arrested and brought to trial. It was a big day. The newspapers were full of the case, every witness was photographed and there was minute and detailed reporting of every word spoken in court. Matt was big news, the centre of attention, but it wasn't a role that he relished. For a while he was confident that the high priced lawyers would see him right, that the detectives would fail in their quest, but gradually he understood that things weren't going his way. The detectives had done their homework, made up for the many times that they had failed to snare their man. This time they had built their chain of evidence. It was hard and unyielding. There were no weak spots. Matt was convicted. The judge, formidable in his righteousness, showed no mercy. Matt was branded a major drugs dealer, a peddler of misery and harm, and sentenced to fifteen years in jail.

Kathleen was devastated, Joey no less so. He hadn't been implicated although the detectives had tried to reel him in as well. But Joey's involvement on this occasion had been minor, the conveying of a few messages. He had never actually handled any drugs and the detectives had to be content with the destruction of his brother. And Matt was destroyed. His business empire fell away, people boycotted his enterprises, shops and pubs were sold, directors in companies in which he had stakes forced him out and hammered his holdings.

Kathleen steeled herself to visit him in jail, waiting self consciously in the dingy hall where visits took place, trying to ignore the stares of the warders and the unfortunate families of other prisoners. In truth no one was really interested. All the men in jail were equal. All had sentences to serve, although few had as long a time of incarceration to contemplate as Matt. Joey went to the prison as well. They had little to say to each other but Joey felt that he had to be there. Matt was silent uncommunicative, introspective. Joey knew that he found his new changed circumstances hard to take. The high flier brought down so unceremoniously. Sheelagh made no visits. On the advice of her family she went to see a solicitor and obtained a separation. Divorce would follow in due course.

Joey's pub was sold and he was unemployed. There was no prospect of another job. No one wanted anything to do with him. He was the brother of a notorious criminal and no one was prepared to take any risks. Joey was confused for a while but soon accepted that this was the way things were and went on the dole. He had no commitments and he got by on the weekly handout.

After the first few months Matt seemed to be in better spirits. He began to talk to Joey and a lot of his old vitality came back. At first Joey wondered why and then he realized that Matt was making his own way in prison. There were opportunities for a wheeler dealer. There were commodities to be traded in, profits of a kind to be made. Matt's status amongst the prison population grew. He became known as the man to connect with when deals were needed. Nothing was beyond his capabilities. The warders watched but didn't interfere. They were understanding men and knew that prisoners had their own necessities, that swapping and trading had its special place in the prison routine and often made things a little easier for men whose prospects were bleak and had very little to give them confidence or respite.

Joey became a courier again, smuggling in the cigarettes and the little packets of drugs that were Matt's stock in trade. He warned Matt about the drugs, but Matt ignored him. If he was caught so what. There was nothing more that they could do to him. He was inside for years and the prison rules held no terrors. The fact that Joey might be caught and imprisoned with him didn't enter his head. He was on a roll again, once more the entrepreneur, the skilful manipulator. He wouldn't make a fortune out of his new enterprises, there would be no pool of cash at the end of the day, but he had other compensations.

Matt became a big man in the prison population. Once again he was a tycoon, looked up to, respected. If a man could become so successful in the forbidding embrace of a prison, what could he do when he regained the outside world. Matt Dillon would rise again. But the warders had other ideas. The drugs trade was becoming too open, causing too much harm. The governor moved and once again Matt was cut down. Even in jail it seemed his talents would never be allowed to flourish unchecked. Success was an elusive, heady thing. Matt had yet to learn that there were no short cuts even for someone as smart as himself. There were rules to be obeyed and those who broke them had to suffer the consequences.

In the world outside Joey counted himself lucky to have escaped. He had learned his lesson. No longer would he be his brother's dogsbody, unquestioningly obeying his every command. He was content to be a nobody, glad that he was not afflicted with his brother's ambition. If success was to be so hard earned then Joey could do without it. Joey was free

162

and could walk around the town. Matt had a different life to lead. But that time would pass. Matt was the brother with the brains. There was always the future.

Joey eventually found a new job. He devoted his spare time to Kathleen who realized that she had made a mistake when she had relied on Matt to care for her in her old age. Joey was steady, reliable. He would become the carer, constant in his love and duty, a success in his own quiet way.

Envy

Megan and Sandra had been friends since school. As children they lived on the same housing estate, went through the tumultuous teenage years together, and got married within weeks of each other. Megan by general consensus married well. Her husband Robert was the son of a local businessman. Sandra married Paddy Joe, a clerk in the county council. Both were bright, keen young men, devoted to their wives and in the course of time to the children which came into their lives. Megan had three, two boys and a girl, and Sandra two, both girls.

Robert bought a house in a new private estate on the outskirts of the town, Paddy Joe and Sandra rented a house from the council. There was no point in working for the council if they didn't get the best they could from the connection, Paddy Joe often said. The council estate was nice enough, the houses plain and unpretentious but they had the great advantage that they were relatively cheap, an important consideration for Paddy Joe since his income was considerably lower than that enjoyed by Robert, who worked in his father's office and would one day take over.

Such promotional prospects were not in line for Paddy Joe. If he stuck at his job, he might one day become a senior clerk, perhaps an official in the planning department but for the moment he was an official in the motor tax office. It was not an inspiring occupation, but Paddy Joe soldiered on, drew down his salary every month and constantly instructed Sandra that she must be frugal in her housekeeping and that a foreign holiday could be undertaken only every second year.

Robert and Megan, on the other hand, when their children were old enough, went abroad twice a year, almost always to Spain where Robert talked about investing in a holiday home. Their house was bright, modern and well furnished, with underfloor electric heating, a conservatory and a large garden.

164

ENVY

They lived well. Megan shopped in the best stores in town, Sandra went to the cheapest supermarket, constantly looked out for special offers and tried to ignore the fact that their furniture was cheap, that their home in comparison to Megan's was definitely an example of social housing. The estate was often rubbish strewn and teenage tearaways left burnt out cars on the green spaces which the council had provided in an effort to encourage its own particular brand of leafy suburbanism.

The apparent difference in their social status made no difference to the young women. They visited each other's homes, the children played together, the friendship of their schooldays translated into a more enduring, mature relationship. Sandra enjoyed her visits to Megan's house. She liked the ambience of the expensive furniture, the deep pile carpets and the increasing collection of pictures which Robert bought from an art dealer he knew in Dublin.

Megan knew nothing of art and took little interest in Robert's purchases, but Sandra had been talented at school and if the money had been available would have gone on to study at the National College of Art and gain a diploma. But it was not to be. She was one of seven children and her father had been a bus driver. Every shilling he earned had gone into the support and care of his family. There was little left over for luxuries and going to college to study art was definitely outside the scope of his pocket. Sandra had gone to work at as a trainee in a local factory and put thoughts of an exciting life as a student in Dublin behind her.

It was when Robert brought home an exciting picture by Jack Yeats that Sandra really felt the first twinge of envy. She was not by nature a jealous person but Megan had really fallen on her feet. Sandra could accept the fact that Robert had a better job than Paddy Joe, that he had bought his wife a better house, and that the holidays abroad and the week-end breaks had become a built in feature of her friend's lifestyle. Sandra shared none of these things. Paddy Joe would never have Robert's financial clout, they would always live in a council house. Their holidays would never amount to more than a week's excursion to Kilkee in Co Clare or Courtown, in Co Wexford.

There was no doubt in Sandra's mind that Megan had done better than herself in life's battle for status and success. But did it have to be so open, so brazen, so wounding.

She went to look at the new picture. It was a seascape, horses in the foreground, cantering on a beach, the waves crashing behind their hooves. Sandra felt that she had never seen so magnificent as these magnificent horses, nor as wild a backdrop. It was the Master at his best.

Robert had hung the painting in the hall, taking down a previously admired painting by Derek Hill. It was now to go above the mantelpiece in the dining room. Sandra stood in the spacious hall way staring at the painting. She could never aspire to owning anything like this. It was something to be prized and flouted as a symbol of affluence, as an indicator that the people who lived in this fine detached house with its large gardens were art lovers, connoisseurs, people of knowledgeable good taste.

The truth was that Robert had known little about art when he started to buy his painting collection. He had learned along the way, accepting his mistakes, his gullability and lack of judgment when it came to value and prices. This Yeats picture had been his best buy yet. It had cost over eighty thousand, but to Robert it was worth every cent. None of his friends could boast of such an acquisition. Its purchase served to whet his appetite, stimulate his ambition to become a renowned collector, a figure of some importance in the art world.

ENVY

There was an article in the local paper about Robert's burgeoning art collection. The reporter who knew nothing of artists, painting and pictures, overwrote the piece. Robert was portrayed as a man of fine distinction with an unrivalled knowledge of the art world, someone who added lustre to the culture of the town.

Sandra read the article in disbelief. She more than anyone else knew that Robert was a philistine, that he invested in paintings and some sculptures too because he had money to spare. His knowledge of art was superficial and his interest driven more by the notoriety of being a collector than any real interest in the work of the artists and the pleasure and piquancy of their paintings.

Robert, however, had a different viewpoint. He began to believe that he had real credentials. That he was a patron. He began to invite young artists from the locality to his home for dinner. Sandra and Paddy Joe were invited too. Robert knew that Sandra had artistic interests of her own. She welcomed these dinners, was delighted to meet people who had persevered with their careers as artists and could rightfully claim to be painters, of whatever merit.

These were bitter sweet occasions, however. As she met more and more of Robert's friends she became more and more conscious of having lost out. If it had not been for her father's difficult financial situation, she too might have been one of these people. Able to talk knowledgeably about their subject, perhaps even to have produced works of merit of her own.

Her attitude to Megan began to change. She still accepted invitations but now seldom reciprocated. Megan now rarely came to her house and their relationship began to trail away. If Megan noticed she said nothing.

167

"Too busy with her own selfish pastimes," Sandra said to her husband "She has no time for me now, with her rich friends, and her airs and graces."

It was in truth an unfair accusation. Megan was by nature trusting and pliant, always with a good word for everyone, always open to suggestions for outings and shopping trips to Dublin. But Sandra, with the increasing financial demands of her growing family, had no spare cash for such activities. Megan could spend in the smart Grafton street stores, and indeed had accounts in some of them, but Sandra never had any money of her own. Every cent of Paddy Joe's salary was earmarked for food, for clothes for her children, for the gas and electricity bills.

Sandra's mood and outlook changed. She became morose, uninterested in her home or Paddy Joe, seldom responding to his suggestions of having a night out in the pub, or going to a play or concert in the local hall. She treated Megan with the same disinterest. Megan was aware that something was amiss. She could sense her friend's dis-satisfaction, and was conscious of the fact that the root of the problem was the difference in social status now separating them. But to Megan, Sandra would always be a friend. That she was well off and lived in a private estate, had her own car, should not be allowed to impact on their relationship. They went back too far.

Megan, astute and understanding realized that her friend was going through a depressive phase. She called on Sandra and urged her to see the doctor, and talked to Paddy Joe as well. But Sandra was obstinate. A few pills would not drive away the growing sense of misery which was engulfing her. She was hostile to Megan and to Paddy Joe and started to blame him for the relatively poor circumstances in which they lived.

In truth Paddy Joe was not doing too badly for his wife and children. A pay round saw him bringing home extra money, he changed the family car, and they went away for a week to Connemara. Sandra seemed in better spirits during the holiday. They stayed in a small hotel and she enjoyed the comparative opulence, the dinners at night, the daytime drives through spectacular countryside. They went to the Connemara pony show at Clifden, it rained, but the children were delighted and drew pictures of ponies and dark mountains for days afterwards.

It was the drawings of the ponies that reminded Sandra of Robert and Megan's wonderful Yeats picture. Try as she might Sandra couldn't get it out of her mind. It epitomized all that was different in her relationship with Megan. Robert had been able to fork out eighty thousand for the painting. The best that Sandra and Paddy Joe could manage was their children's jerky sketches of the ponies of the west of Ireland. It was too much. Something would have to change in their lives. She couldn't go on like this, second rate, struggling on Paddy Joe's woefully inadequate salary, permanently condemned to life on a council estate.

It was their surroundings now which perturbed Sandra most. Megan had her beautiful house with its lawns and occasional fruit trees. Sandra and her family lived in a boxy dingy house which was totally indistinguishable from the houses which surrounded it. Sandra felt that she was condemned to a moribund existence, with no easement of their situation, no way out.

Paddy Joe worried about Sandra's moods, consulted his friends and was told that it was her time of life. She would get over it. Everyone of his friends had gone through some sort of difficulty with their marriage. He had to live with it until it was over. Paddy Joe did his best, but more and more he went to the pub after work, spending more of the money which already was so hard to stretch over the household bills. If

Sandra noticed what was going on she took no notice. She was no longer interested in her husband's company. He couldn't give her what she wanted, a new house, new possessions, an art collection which would rival that of Robert.

She kept the children's drawings and in the hours when they were at school pored over them at the kitchen table, contrasting their straggling lines and colours with the flair and beauty of the Yeats painting which hung in Robert and Megan's hallway. It was a shame, she told herself. They had everything. She had nothing, only a few unformed drawings completed by her children. It was no consolation for the magnificent prize in her friends' house.

One day when she could stand it all no longer, she tore up the children's drawings and threw the pieces in the bin. Then she went into the living room and lay down on the sofa, crying bitterly. It was all so unfair. Megan had been her friend and confidant for many years. Schooldays and romantic liaisons had passed them by unscathed, but now when both their lives were settled there was a gulf, a chasm which could not be bridged.

She got up and raged around the room, mounting anger taking charge. Everyone became a target, Paddy Joe, her children, Robert and Megan, life itself.

Rational thoughts tried desperately to overcome her plunge into depression. There were good things in life, she counselled herself. She had a faithful husband. They did not really lack for anything. But then the dark thoughts took over. Megan had so much more. It was so unfair.

Sandra's breakdown continued over several months. If Paddy Joe noticed anything amiss he said nothing. He too was beginning to feel a change in the relationship with his wife. There was nothing for him at home. The sessions in the pub grew longer. The children were bemused, too young to comprehend what was happening in their lives, sensing that things were not as they should be but unable to exercise any influence over the direction of events.

Sandra made no effort to pull herself together. There was one focus of her thoughts and that was Megan. Megan the beneficiary of all that was good in life. The contrast between herself and her friend became more impacted on her tortured mind. There had been so little difference between them as youngsters growing up. They had shared the same ideals, reveled in the same songs and music, laboured over the same romances that hallmarked their teenage years. Why now were things so different.

Sandra allowed her dishevelled thoughts to dominate her days. Gradually she focused on Megan as the source of her unhappiness. The Yeats picture in her hallway figured strongly in her bemused assesssment of her situation. It was the picture which had brought about the final break up. Without it, Megan had been her friend, her best friend, the physical differences in their lives overcome by the years of acceptance of each other's foibles, shortcomings and occasional achievements.

There was only one course of action. With the children at school, and Paddy Joe at work, Sandra left the house and walked the mile or so to Megan's house. She paused at the gate and stared unseeingly at her surroundings. The lawns were freshly mowed, the front door newly painted. Inside she could hear the sound of a vacuum cleaner. Megan's cleaning lady was at work. Sandra had picked her moment. She knew that Megan would be out, morning coffee with friends at one of the chic restaurants in the town was one of the fixtures of her day.

She went to the back door and pushed it open. The vacuuming was taking place upstairs. There was no one else in the house.

She walked through the kitchen and into the hallway and stood in front of the picture. She had often admired its beauty, its awe inspiring capture of the magnificence of the horses and the crescendo of the waves on the shore. Today she had no time for such admiration. Today the found the painting ugly, a symbol of her torment. It should not be hanging there. Robert should not have bought it, paying out all that money. For a second or two she allowed her thoughts to dwell on what she would have done with such a large amount. But she found no solace in such contemplation.

She put up a hand and fingered the ornate gilded frame. It had come with the painting. Robert had said that it wasn't suitable, that he would get something simpler. But he had not found the time to find an alternative, so the masterpiece had remained in its surround, magnificent, but still not quite comfortable in its ambience.

Sandra too found the frame unsuitable. Instinctively, all her latent artistic talents suddenly brought to the fore, she agreed with Robert's assessment. But why hadn't he done something about it. Why had he allowed the painting to remain esconced in such unsuitable attire. She blamed him for arrogance, for indifference to the painting's integrity. He had bought a plaything, an ornament. He did not deserve to have such a wonderful possession.

The vacuum cleaner upstairs was switched off and footsteps sounded on the landing. Suddenly alarmed, Sandra made her way hurriedly back through the kitchen and into the garden. In her hurry to escape she knocked over a chair. She ignored the footsteps behind her and ran for the gate and was gone. Behind her the cleaning lady opened the front door and looked out. There was nothing to see, no one was there. Confused the woman went back inside and picked up the kitchen chair. Someone had been in the kitchen she felt sure. She locked the kitchen door and continued with her household duties. When her employer returned she would tell her about the incident, conveying a warning that someone might be contemplating robbing the house.

Sandra spent the rest of the day in a daze. She wasn't at all clear about what she had intended to do, but at the back of her mind was the realization that it would have been a step too far. She hated Robert's painting, she hated Robert and Megan too, and all their family. She hated the life to which she herself was condemned, as she saw it, an empty, meaningless life totally devoid of purpose or well being.

By teatime she had made up her mind. This time she would carry out the threat which loomed in her mind. The painting stood between herself and Megan. It was an intruder. It had to be destroyed. Good relations would resume once the picture had been removed from its place of honour in her friends' house. Megan would thank her in the end. She would realize that Sandra had no alternative, that the restoration of good relations between them was more important than any picture on the wall, no matter how beautiful, how valuable.

It was dark when Sandra left the house once more. The clocks had gone back several weeks before and the early shades of winter were drawing in. She shivered in the cold night air and for a moment nearly gave up and went back into the comfort of her home. But the restless, eager, thrust of her thoughts took hold again and she walked on. It was easy to get into Megan's house. The kitchen door was unlocked as usual and she hurried into the hall. The house seemed to be empty, its owners somewhere in the town.

She stared up at the picture for a moment or to, scraped her fingers across the oiled layers of its outlines and realized that she had brought no means of accomplishing its destruction. She went back out to the kitchen and took a knife from the cutlery drawer. Then back out into the hall. She slashed at the

173

painting tearing away the severed strips of canvas and throwing them down at her feet. In less than a minute it was all over. The picture was in tatters, destroyed for ever. A sense of triumph, of exultation, swept over her.

Then came remorse. Suddenly she realised the enormity of what she had done. It was a terrible thing. Megan and Robert would never forgive her. There could be no rational explanation, no excuse. However well presented, nothing she could say would exonerate her from this needless orgy of destruction. She had ravaged a beautiful thing, a prized possession. There was no way back. Instead of mending her fractured relationship with Megan she had torn it down forever.

She began to cry. Hot tears coursed down her cheeks and she stumbled blindly out into the night. She had only one thought now. To get away. To distance herself entirely from what had happened. No one must know that she had been here. The destruction of the painting must remain an unsolved mystery. Perhaps it could be blamed on one of the children, perhaps on some mindless vandal who had come into the house in search of plunder, found nothing and taken out his rage on the nearest available thing of beauty.

As she got nearer to home she began to consider a different strategy. The terrible thing she had done must never be discovered. There was only one way out. Fire! That was the answer. She would burn down Megan's house and cover up her deed. The enormity of what she was doing did not cross her mind. Everything now was concentrated on hiding all trace of her savage act. She went to the garage where Paddy Joe kept his Volvo at night and picked up the can of petrol he kept for emergencies. Then she was off again, stumbling through the darkness, half running, half walking, the can banging heavily against her legs.

Into the house again and across the kitchen to the hall. There was still no sign of any occupant. She splashed the petrol on the carpeted stairway, tossing the can aside. Now she had no light. Back into the kitchen and a quick rummage for matches. A box was found and she was back in the hall way in seconds. She struck match after match and tossed them on the doused stair carpet and banisters. A great roll of fire swept up towards the ceiling. Sandra stared at the flames for a moment, transfixed then she ran out of the house, leaving the billowing furnace behind her.

Half way home she turned and look back. Sparks were flying into the sky over Megan's house, and there was a glow from the windows. It was well alight. Her terrible secret would not be uncovered. No one would know that she had slashed the painting. She was safe now. Her friendship with Megan could resume. There was nothing to come between them.

A fire engine swept past, its siren screaming. Then another. It must be a big fire, she thought to herself, or why would they send two units. She got home and went to the bathroom. Her face was black from smoke and her hair was singed. She tidied herself up and went down stairs to make herself a cup of coffee. Paddy Joe and the kids would be in soon. She must be calm, give nothing away. As far as anyone was concerned she had never been out of the house.

She was laying the table for supper when she realized with a start that she had overlooked one important item. She had thrown down the petrol can when it was empty and left it lying in Megan's hallway. Panic momentarily set in. Paddy Joe would miss the can at some stage. Frantically she racked her mind for an excuse, but nothing came. Then she dismissed her concern. It could be months before her husband noticed that it was missing. By then everything would be forgotten.

She sat at the table waiting for her family to return. She was

175

making toasted cheese for supper. It was their favourite snack at night. The kids would wolf the slices down and she would stand beside the cooker laying out the strips of cheese and toasting them on the grill. They were late. What was keeping them. Finally the car drew up outside and the children came in. Paddy Joe was a few steps behind them. The kids were unusually quiet, there was no jostling, no rancour, no expressions of delight that supper was ready. Paddy Joe's face was grave.

He took his wife by the arm and pressed her into a seat.

"I've bad news," he said sombrely.

"There's been an accident. It's Megan. Her house went on fire. She was upstairs and couldn't get out in time. The firemen were too late. The whole house went up. She had no chance."

Sandra sat in silence. For a while no tears came but then she began to cry. Paddy Joe tried to comfort her, but Sandra was beyond consolation. Megan was gone and their friendship was terminated forever. Paddy Joe thought he understood and tried to console. But Sandra would not be comforted. She had a ghastly secret. It would haunt her forever. She would always remember the vivid, exuberant, cantering horses on the seashore that had hung on Megan's wall. She had loved and hated them and envied Megan for having such a thing of beauty in her home. Now all that was gone and Sandra was left with her thoughts, her destructive envy finally driven from her mind to be replaced with a terrible remorse.

Romance

Belfast had changed. Everyone said so. The city centre was bright and cheerful. The soldiers were off the streets. There was no car bomb rubble. The shops were big windowed, full of designer clothes, expensive furniture and luxury goods. People stayed out late in the evenings. The pubs and wine bars were full, restaurants and bistros busy. New buildings were going up everywhere. Belfast had come alive again. The people were friendly, communicative, the old sores no longer in evidence.

Yes, Belfast had changed. It was a place for young people now. People who remembered little about the war. People who had things to do. They had ambitions, prospects, solutions. Religion and politics no longer impacted with the blunt force of the old days.

In the working class suburbs life was not that different. The old animosities were not far from the surface. A hard core stayed entrenched in the shrinking ghettos. Murals, flags and painted kerbstones still testified to the existence of old allegiances, old hatreds. Paramilitaries, stripped of the need for bomb making and gunfire, turned to drugs and extortion to fuel their passions, their creeds endorsed by beatings and shootings. There were those who approved. The police made little impact on the robbers and hooligans who flourished in a culture which gave little support to law and order. If people were punished they had only themselves to blame.

They met in one of the city centre bars that catered for all sides of the divide. Someone introduced them. She was Marina Harding. He was William Kennedy. They had neutral names, his deliberately so. In reality he was Liam Kennedy from Andersonstown, but he told her that he was from Dungannon. He wasn't sure about her. She just said she was from Belfast and left it at that. There was nothing to indicate whether she was Protestant or Catholic. She was a lively, fresh

177

faced, laughing person, an attractive young woman who clearly had a zest for life and was interested in male companionship. She was twentyone, and was a civil servant. She worked at Stormont, one of the thousands of people who provided the back up for the newly booming province. Liam was two years older, worked in a solicitor's office and was soon to take his final examinations which would qualify him as a barrister. They were educated, modern young people on good salaries who intended to make the most of life.

Liam had a flat near the university. He brought her there after their third date. He checked his possessions carefully beforehand. There was nothing to indicate either his religion or his political allegiances. No Irish history books, no republican emblems, no religious symbols, nothing that would in any way cause concern to his visitor. He still wasn't sure about her. Carefully loaded questions had produced no results. Her first name Marina was unusual for a Catholic, but like her surname Harding, could have been from either camp. There were many familial names in Northern Ireland which had crossed the divide. Kennedy was a similar instance. There were Kennedys on both sides. Liam would have been a complete giveaway, but William - well William was the name of the victor at the Boyne and had its own particular resonance if one was Protestant and Unionist.

Liam had no political leanings. He had been twelve when the cease fire was called and had no real memories of the violence. His parents of course were staunchly republican and voted for Sinn Fein at every election. But their home, deep in nationalist West Belfast, had been spared the attentions of the military, and the bitterness of the conflict had made little direct impact on the family. His father worked locally, all their relations were in the area, and they seldom went outside the district. Running the gauntlet of the Shankill road to get to the city centre was too risky. West Belfast was self sufficient and the Kennedys were amongst their own people. Like all their neighbours they hated the British and the roaming Protestant murder gangs, but had no confrontations with either.

Things had settled down when it was time for Liam to go to Queens and study law. Queens was a friendly environment. The Catholics had taken over, unionists were in a minority, and the legal profession particularly was the focus of Catholic ambition. Education was the weapon of the Catholic working classes and the days when his co-religionists were cowed, unemployed, and ground down by a hostile state apparatus were gone. Life for Liam Kennedy was promising. He had no doubt that he would become a successful barrister, that he would marry and settle down in a smart house in one of the new leafy suburbs that were springing up around the city.

Their romance prospered. They had got to the stage when they met two or three evenings during the week and Marina often stayed over at week-ends. They were avid clubbers and patrons of bistros around the center of the city. Liam lived his masquerade as a Protestant easily. He didn't feel like a Catholic. He had left Catholic attitudes behind him when he left West Belfast and set up his flat near Queens. He had Protestant and Catholic friends and in the new dispensation that was gradually emerging in the province and felt that he was under no compulsion to project a loyalty to any particular allegiance.

The relationship survived a few upheavals. Marina was sometimes inclined to be over possessive, but it was an attitude formed from love. Liam sometimes was casual, offhanded, and she responded with a little fire, but mostly they were compliant, content lovers, happy in their pursuit of each other, certain in their commitment.

Eventually Marina raised the issue of bringing him home to meet her family. Her father was a redundant shipyard worker, her mother fitted in part time hours in a nearby newsagents, and there were two brothers, Sam and Davy. Sam was long term unemployed but Davey worked as a binman with the Corporation. At twenty four and nineteen respectively both seemed content with their lot. Both gave their mother something for the housekeeping but both had cash to spend, Sam a little less than Davey. The local pubs were well supported, and Sam had a role in the local unit of the UVF.

It was when Marina finally gave up her family's address that Liam realized the predicament he was in. The Hardings lived in one of the backstreets off the Shankill road. They were Protestant to the core and Liam knew that irrespective of the relationship which he had forged with the daughter of the house he would not be welcome there if it became known that he was a Catholic.

He was in deep with Marina. They were as close as any young couple could get, and Liam was inches away from asking her to move in with him permanently. His flat was too small for two people living together on a full time basis, but he had some money set aside. They could rent a bigger flat or even a house without too much difficulty, and he knew that with their combined salaries it would be possible to take out a mortgage and buy a home.

These thoughts had been in his mind for some time. He had tentatively broached the subject of setting up together on a couple of occasions and Marina, while not exactly jumping at the proposal, had not shot it down out of hand. But now there was a problem. She wanted contact with her family and it was only a matter of time before she brought him home. He was sorry now that he had said that he was from Dungannon, but he knew that if he had confessed to hailing from Andersonstown at the start of their relationship it would have gone nowhere.

180

ROMANCE

He had never actually said that he was not a Protestant but it had been implied. Neither of them had any interest in politics or evinced any sympathy for one side or the other, but the division while hidden was there nonetheless. Liam worried over the issue for several days and decided that he must come clean. It was only a matter of time before she would have to know. There was no question of marriage and church appearances. Young people these days had no interest in marriage and neither of them were churchgoers. But there was a chasm between them. Somehow, even if it meant risking the whole relationship, Liam knew that he had to put Marina in the picture.

A meeting with her family came up before Liam had an opportunity to set the record straight. She sprang it on him one evening after work when they were having a drink together in one of the neutral bars that abounded in the city centre. Every pub still had its doormen, but the days of the drive by shootings were long over. Mainstream pubs, owned mainly by Catholics, were no longer targets and people could drink where they liked. People deliberately avoided politics and diversity was kept below the surface. Instinctively they knew by each others' names what people were. But religion and politics were still major issues for the older generation and Liam Kennedy had to seriously confront them for the first time.

"I have to go home this evening," she told him. "I haven't seen mam for weeks. She rang me last night and I promised I would bring you as well."

Liam was caught out. Several times over the past few weeks he had been tempted to bring up the subject of his religion but circumstances had not been opportune. Now he was caught out. He could not refuse to go, but now that he knew where she lived, he realized that he could not admit what he was. For one thing it would be too much a shock for Marina. She needed time for preparation, for assimilation of the knowledge, for assessment of the situation. For another thing, he knew that he would not be welcomed by Marina's family if his secret came out.

He tried to make an excuse not to go, but she was having none of it.

"I want you to meet the folks," she said. "It's time they got to know you. I've told them all about you but they want to see for themselves. I'm proud of you and I want them to be proud as well."

Liam realised that there was a pragmatism behind her words. An up and coming young barrister was a good catch for a girl from a working class home off the Shankill road. If they eventually got married it would be a step up for Marina and her family. But religion was a running sore. It would be a total disaster if she married a Catholic.

He went along with her wishes and they set off for the Shankill together. A bus brought them to within a few streets of their destination and they got off to walk the rest of the way. It was summer time and the bunting flew from house to house. The kerb stones had been newly painted in red white and blue and there were loyalist murals on the table ends. This was loyalist heartland. A different people lived here. Only a couple of miles away there were different flags, different paintwork, different murals. Different gangs of subversives controlled the streets, the drugs trade was in different hands, and punishment beatings were carried out by different people.

It was all too familiar to Liam. He had been brought up in the fractious atmosphere of his own particular ghetto. His people were Irish. These people were British. They flew Union Jacks where up the Falls and into Andersonstown they flew the Tricolour. The heroes were different, the commemorations

182

also. The Somme was the iconic fixture in loyalist Belfast. The Easter Rising and the Hunger Strikes were the glorious memories of the republican heartland.

Marina's parents were both at home when they arrived. Tom Harding spent most of his days in front of the television. Occasionally he went down to one of the loyalist pubs that catered for the drinking necessities of the district. He had spent all his life in the shipyard and had no prospect of further work when he was laid off.

He wasn't embittered by the experience and now at just over sixty he was enjoying his retirement. The shipyard work had been well paid, but back breaking, and he relished the thought that he no longer had to get up at six every morning and head off to handle ice cold rivets and rigid sheets of heavy metal.

He welcomed Liam with a strong handshake and an invitation to a drop of whiskey. Marina's aproned mother, Margaret, came in from the kitchen where she had been making soda bread. They were kind, friendly, sociable people and Liam warmed to them right away.

He knew where he was, however. There was a picture of the Queen on the wall over the fireplace and an Orange collarette was slung over the back of the sofa. It would be in constant use at this time of year, Liam reflected. Lodge meetings and local band parades leading up to the big parade on the Twelfth were a fact of life in this deeply loyal remnant of Empire.

Marina and her mother withdrew to the tiny kitchen to gossip and Liam was left in the sitting room with her father. They talked about football, the premiership, the prospects for Northern Ireland in the World Cup qualifying sequence. Liam was knowledgeable about both soccer and Gaelic football and conversed easily with his host. Margaret Harding brought in a tray of tea things and cheese on toast and they wolfed the offerings down.

Their conversation was interrupted with the arrival of Marina's eldest brother Sam. Liam introduced himself.

"Bill Kennedy,' he said easily and clasped the outstretched hand.

Sam Harding was very much a product of the Shankill. Tall, muscular and overweight, he had tattoos on both arms and a loyalist mural on his teeshirt. His head was shaven and he had a fat Alsatian on a leash. Liam stroked the dog's head and the overweight canine responded.

Tom Harding laughed.

"You'll get on well with us," he said. "The dog likes you. You'll do."

Liam laughed in turn and they talked on. At one stage Tom suggested a trip to the pub, but Liam declined. He had to get back to the far side of the city, he explained. It would take at least an hour and a half. Marina came out from the kitchen, ready to go. They got up, said their goodbyes, and left. Tom Harding and his wife followed them to the door.

"Well, that wasn't too bad now was it" Marina asked. "You got on well with Dad. I could tell. He liked you. Mam thinks you're gorgeous."

Liam laughed. The evening had gone well and he was pleased. Marina's parents were friendly, decent people, much like his own. There was a hidden void, of course, but that was the way things were. He wished that Belfast was not such a riven city. Why should religion dominate their lives so much. It would be better if there was no religion, if everyone went to school together and everyone was either Protestant or Catholic, not so bitterly divided.

The next day Liam decided to visit his own family. The buses were running to Andersonstown without interruption now and he made the journey in under an hour. His parents were glad to see him. It had been nearly a year, although he had made regular phone calls. The Kennedys in most respects were a mirror for Marina's people. Their circumstances were similar, they were working class but had succeeded in getting Liam to Queens, just as Marina had left her home environment behind her and got a job with the civil service. Their children were both examples of the new generation of young people, educated, articulate, ready to some extent to leave the past behind but in many ways still curtailed by its factionism and tribal loyalties.

They were having tea when Liam decided to break the news.

"I've found a girl," he said haltingly. "We're going to try and make something of ourselves." Eileen Kennedy's face lit up. She wanted Liam to get married but he had brought very few girls home. This was the first time in fact that he had confessed to having any kind of stable relationship.

"Who is she, son," his father asked eagerly. "What does she do."

"Her name is Marina Harding and she works at Stormont – in the civil service" Liam replied.

"Harding." His father mused over the name. "Is she from Belfast."

"She's from the Shankill," Liam admitted awkwardly. "We've been going out together for over a year now."

"The Shankill!" Eileen Kennedy's voice rose sharply. "What

are you saying."

"She's a Protestant, ma," he said slowly. "But it makes no difference. We don't think anything of such things now. Times have changed. "

"Some things never change," his father said slowly. "You can't be serious about settling down with a Protestant girl. It won't work out. You'll see. Her own family will be totally against it. You'll cause trouble there. Do they know about you."

Liam admitted that they didn't. "We haven't told them yet," he said. "I've met them, but I wanted you to know first. Marina doesn't care and nor do I. We love each other. That's what is important."

He wondered briefly if in fact this accurately reflected Marina's outlook. He hadn't told her yet. She had just assumed that he was one of her own. What would her reaction be.

His father caught the indecision in his face.

"You haven't told her," he accused his son.

For a moment Liam was going to deny the accusation but he decided that there was no point.

"I'm going to tell her this evening," he said. "But it won't make any difference. She thinks like me. This religion thing is done away with. We're different now."

"Are you going to get married," Eileen asked quietly. "What are your plans."

Liam shrugged.

186

"Marriage isn't as important as it used to be either," he said. "Young people live together now. It's the way things are."

"It's not the way things are round here," his father said brusquely. "The priests are dead set against people shacking up together. They won't have it and they won't have you marrying a Protestant girl either."

Liam shrugged again.

"My mind is made up,' he said. "If we decided to get married we can got to a registry office. We don't have to have it done in church."

A tear rolled down Eileen's cheek.

"You must do whatever you think is best," she said. "We won't stand in your way but you need to be very sure of what you're doing."

His father grunted and turned the pages of his newspaper.

They spent a few minutes more together and then Liam left. They parted on an awkward note. This was a Catholic household. The Sacred Heart lamp in the hall and the pictures of the 1916 leaders on the living room wall testified to that. The Kennedys and the Hardings were different people. Nothing could change that situation. People had tried before but things had always worked out badly. Couples in mixed marriages had been ostracized by their communities, sometimes even burned out of their homes.

His mother stood in the doorway to see him off. A Corporation refuse lorry was parked a few yards away. The bin men were doing their thing with the rubbish. A second truck entered the street. This was the recycling lorry. The houses had different coloured bins for the stuff that was intended for the dump and the items that were destined for recycling. Liam passed them by. It was a familiar scene. He thought nothing of it.

Miranda brought him out to visit her parents again the following evening. He was welcomed, everyone was friendly and this time Miranda's younger brother Davey was at home. They called him Billy and treated him as a fully fledged member of the family. Marina had not been backward in expressing her commitment to him and her family had fully accepted that this was the man with whom she intended to have a long term relationship.

It was Davey who struck a different note. After the first few moments of introduction he was staring sharply at Liam, focused, almost as if he disbelieved that Billy was really his sister's boyfriend.   Liam knew instinctively that something was wrong. Davey was distant, withdrawn, suspicious.

Crunch time came about half an hour later. They were having cups of tea in the sitting room and Liam was biting heavily into one of Margaret's scones.

Davey Harding suddenly broke his silence. His face was flushed, his manner now outrightly hostile.

"I've seen you before," he burst out. "You live in Andersonstown. I was at your house yesterday with the bins. You're a Taig, a goddam Shinner."

He jumped up and lunged towards Liam who immediately vacated his chair and put up his hands to defend himself.

"Here. None of that," Tom Harding interposed, at a loss, confused, at the sudden turn of events.

"He's a Shinner," Davey shouted again. "Our sister is going

188

out with a Catholic."

He bunched his fists and went to have a go at Liam. Tom Harding got between them. Marina and her mother came in from the kitchen. They had heard everything. Marina's face was white, her whole body tensed.

They stood in silence for a few moments. Then Marina spoke.

"Is it true,' she asked. Tell me the truth. I thought you were one of us. Tell me Davey's wrong."

Liam shook his head.

"It's true," he said disconsolately. "I was going to tell you one of these days. It make's no difference," he went on urgently. "We love each other. Religion won't split us up."

"I'm damn sure it will," Tom Harding said harshly. "There is no way our daughter is going to take up with a Catholic. It's over. Leave this house and don't come back."

Liam looked pleadingly at Marina. She was ashen, her body shaking a little now, not far from tears. He moved towards her. She put out a hand to push him back.

"Out" Davey shouted, repeating his father's injunction. "Get out now and don't come back."

Liam left. There was nothing else he could do. The door banged behind him and he could hear raised voices from inside the house. Davey was berating his sister. Her parents evidently were saying nothing. Liam had caught a glimpse of Margaret's face as he left. She was devastated, her hopes for her daughter now cruelly cast down. Liam knew that they had liked him. The sudden turnaround in their attitude was hard to take. He was in love with Marina. Why should this have to come between them.

There was no word from Marina for the next few days. Liam
went to work as usual but stayed in his flat in the evenings
wanting to be there in case Marina had a change of heart. He
tried her on her mobile phone dozens of times but it was shut
down. His own was silent too. It seemed as if all was lost. A
terrible gulf had fractured their love. Liam was in real pain.
His love for Marina had been all consuming. Not for one
moment had he believed that their different religions would
divide them. Subconsciously he had known it was a problem,
but he had convinced himself that they would understand each
other, that their feelings would overcome this tribal division.

On the third night Marina came to his flat. She was ragged,
her eyes dark and red from crying. He took her in his arms and
kissed her gently. For a few moments she made no response,
but then she gave her answer. Their love was greater than the
outlook of their families. She wanted him and was prepared to
make the necessary sacrifices.

"You should have told me sooner," she remonstrated. "I would
have prepared them for it. They wouldn't really go against me.
But I wasn't ready. I had no idea. Why didn't you tell me."

"I didn't want to lose you," Liam answered emotionally. "I
would have told you in time. I had made up my mind to do it. I
told my own family a few days ago. They were just as hostile
as yours."

They sat in silence on the sofa.

"What are we going to do," Marina asked eventually. "We're
at a dead end."

"We have to go on together in spite of our families," Liam
answered definitely. "They'll come around in time."

ROMANCE

At that moment there was a knock on the door. Liam got up to answer it. He had barely taken off the latch when the door was thrown back in his face. Sam Harding with two other men behind him burst into the room. They were carrying baseball bats.

Marina screamed and tried to interpose herself between her brother and Liam. It was no use. Sam Harding struck out with the bat and hit Liam across the face. He went down, almost unconscious. They kicked and beat him for several minutes. Liam put up his arms to protect his head and they responded with a renewed assault on his body. Marina screamed and screamed. Then it was all over. Liam was bloody and unconscious on the floor. The raiders were gone. They bundled Marina out with them. Liam lay on the floor alone broken, battered.

He went to the hospital the following morning. One of his neighbours aroused by the fighting had administered some rudimentary first aid in the mean time. Liam had gone to bed, sick, sore bruised and bleeding from a cut on his head. His face was a mass of mottled bruising. People looked at him curiously as he waited for attention in the A and E unit but he ignored them. The doctor and the nurses were indifferent. Such incidents were commonplace in Belfast. It was part of the city's lifestyle. People had been brought in who were in a much worse state than Liam Kennedy.

He went back to his flat, patched up, still in pain but with most of his suffering eased with tablets. He lay down on the bed and wallowed in his misery. The Hardings had made their views on his association with their sister quite plain. Theirs was not a romance which had any future. Next time things might be much worse. He might even be killed. Sam Harding was a product of his place and era. He could expect no mercy. He felt pain for Marina and pain for his loss and pain for his injuries. Life for Liam Kennedy suddenly had little meaning.

191

Marina came back that evening. She was carrying a small flight bag and had a determined air.

"We've got to go," she said. "We can't stay here. It's not safe. We'll never have a future in this city. We must leave it all behind."

Liam looked at her dazedly.

"You mean you still want me," he asked.

She smiled at him.

"Of course I do," she said quietly. "Nothing will come between us. But we've got to get out. Tonight. For good."

Obediently he packed a few things in a suitcase and followed her down the stairs to the street. He flinched for a moment in the doorway, fear that someone might be lurking there momentarily taking control. But she pulled him on. They got a taxi to the airport. She already had their flights booked. He marveled silently at her resourcefulness and then allowed himself to be caught up in events.

They sat side by side in the airplane. He had the seat nearest the window. She thrust a hand into his as the plane taxied down the runway and took off into the night sky. He looked down at the vanishing lights of the city. A new life lay before them, but what did the future hold. Would their love sustain them through difficult years ahead. They were running now, absorbed, united, and confident in their flight. But sometime the running had to stop. Would they remain strong for each other, or would the instinctive pull of their homes, families, and different loyalties, draw them back to Belfast, separated, alone.

Pride

"You just have to take it easy. Kick wide. Make sure there's no advantage. No one will know."

"I'll know" Con O'Malley said grimly. "And someone is bound to figure it out. People are not fools. They know my form."

"You can have an off day," Evan Jordan said. "You're entitled to that."

The bookie sat back in his seat and fingered the ignition key. He waited for a further remonstrance from the team captain but O'Malley had run out of argument.

Jordan smiled grimly. He knew his man. O'Malley was too far into him to have any real fire in his belly. That was the way with compulsive gamblers. They were often good at what they did, but it was superficial. When the going got tough they caved in. Jordan knew that O'Malley would see things his way. The footballer had no option. It was either throw the match or face the consequences. Jordan had made it plain what those consequences would be. The heavies would come calling and O'Malley would be in hospital for months.

The footballer sighed and slowly got out of the car. Jordan started the engine and nonchalantly waved a farewell hand and drove off, satisfied that he had got his message through. There was a lot of money riding on the county final. Jordan had laid O'Malley's team to lose. The punters had scented victory and big money had been wagered.

On form, losing was an unlikely eventuality. O'Malley's men had a long track record of victory, O'Malley himself was the star of the side, and had never let them down. At least two goals could be expected to fly off his boot and with the backup of an aggressive forward line up could be counted upon to carry the day. A defeat was not only unlikely but to many, the majority in fact, unthinkable. Thousands of pounds had been wagered on the result. Jordan's offer had been derided in every pub in the town. The bookie stood to lose thousands if Stoneyford Gaels won the cup, but the end result was down to Con O'Malley. He alone could bring the whole thing crashing down. He had to be stopped and Jordan was not the man to flinch from difficult or dangerous alternatives.

Con lived for two things. His family and football. Michelle, his wife, often said that football, overshadowed everything, that the lads at the club were more important than herself, their two sons, Cian and Cormac, and that if the choice ever had to be made, Con would abandon his family in favour of the tall goal posts and muddy pitch. It was an exaggeration, of course. Michelle had a case for sometimes believing that she was secondary in Con's life, but the reality was that his family came first. Their sons far outranked anything that football could offer. Con was proud of both of them. They too in the course of time would become great footballers, he was certain. As a father he was giving them a lot to live up to, but there was no doubt in his mind that the O'Malley name would be part of Stoneyford Gaels for many years to come.

Con O'Malley was a stylish, elegant footballer. He was known and widely respected for his clean play, his adherence to the rules, his tough but fair dealings on and off the pitch. The rules were what counted, he often told his friends. If you didn't play by them you shouldn't play at all. You had to have respect for the game, your team and your opponents. Play hard, play tough but play fair. There were footballers who used the game to work off their aggression, but Con O'Malley wasn't one of these. He had never raised his fist to strike a man or used his boot to bring a man down. He played by the rules and expected everyone else to do the same.

Critics said that at thirty two it was time for Con to hang up his boots, but in fact he had never played better. He was in his prime, operated a fitness and healthy eating regime that was the envy of the younger players, and held on to his captain's role, not for anything he had done in the past, but by sheer determination, a will to play his part, an ability founded on experience, and a zest for the game itself.

Con O'Malley was captain because he deserved to be. He reinforced his grip on the post every time he played, and more than anyone else had driven the team year after year to the county final. Sometimes they took the cup, sometimes they were defeated by a narrow margin, but whatever the outcome, Con O'Malley's sportsmanship shone through. He was a role model for every young lad in the parish and the time would come when he would have the same influence over his sons.

Con never doubted that both of them would become top class footballers in their own right. The urge to follow their father was already there to be seen. Michelle brought them to all the matches, Cian the eldest at seven, and Cormac only two years behind him, clapped and cheered at every move their father made. They led the plaudits when Con scored a goal and recognized the excellence of the play that so often set up his team mates to shoot into the net or over the bar. Con told them about the rules and made sure that even at this early stage they understood what sportsmanship was all about. His boys when they went out to play as juniors in a few years time would be as honest and clean in their play as their father. This would be his legacy, ensuring that they gave their best but that they always should respect for the game, for their team and for their opponents.

Con's weakness was gambling. He had been a client of Evan Jordan for years, first as an over the counter customer, then as an account holder. He would back on anything, horses, dogs, the Premiership, international rugby. Sometimes he won, more often he lost, but the occasional wins fuelled his lust.   Losses had to be regained. Wins only spurred him on to greater excesses. It had taken over a year for Con to get so far into the bookie that there was no way out.

Con owed thousands. Evan had never cramped his style. His credit was always good, but in his heart Con knew that something would have to be done. Somehow he would have to get out of Evan Jordan's clutches. Somehow he would have to get himself free of the treacherous, clinging, suffocating, snake that enveloped him. Con realized that he had an addiction as bad or perhaps even worse than that which afflicted other men. Their downfall was drink, drugs, or even women, but Con's malady on the surface was clean and non debilitating, but the reality was that his whole life was under threat. His wages went nowhere, his mortgage payments fell behind, his car was several years out of date, there wasn't enough money to pay for outings for Michelle and the kids.

Evan Jordan played Con like a fish under the Mayfly. He kept Con's meagre payments coming in with an occasional discreet word, said nothing when a win reduced the overall amount of his indebtedness and carefully watched his man. He knew that short of selling up his home, Con could never pay off his gambling debts. Because he ran an account Con didn't even have the satisfaction of getting his winnings into his hand. There was always a big balance due.

Once or twice, Con had transferred to other bookies, but Evan had been alert and warned him that that this was a course that was not open to him. If Con wanted to move his custom then would have to settle up, and this was something that was quite beyond his capabilities. Con O'Malley was well and truly hooked. Unless something extraordinary occurred, a win on the Lotto perhaps, or a legacy from a relation, there was no escape.

In a way, Jordan's proposition had come as a relief. At last

196

there was the chance of getting out of his troubles. But the whole concept of deliberately throwing a match, of undercutting his team mates, was something from which Con O'Malley shrank. He was under no illusions, once Evan Jordan had pushed him down this road there was no going back. Jordan would have him in his grip, irrespective of the amount of his debts. And this wouldn't get him totally out of debt. It would clear the most of it, but there would be a margin left over, enough to ensure that Con was back in thrall, gambling again to get clear, building up his losses until he was the bookie's creature once again.

The thought of what he had to do overshadowed Con's life in the days leading up to the match. His tortured mind was divorced even from the need to place a bet. What if things went wrong. What if people saw through his attempts to divert the course of play. Worse again what if all his efforts failed to change the outcome. It was possible, although perhaps unlikely, for Stoneyford Gaels to win without their captain's input. But the spectators would be expecting Con to shine as usual. Spectacular feats would be demanded. It was the way he had performed in other finals. Con was the key man, the leader who would seize the fleeting advantages, score the elusive point that determined the outcome.

He had played better than ever this season, partly from escapism, the need to get away from the pit into which he had fallen, partly from an urge to demonstrate that irrespective of his age, he was still a force to be reckoned with, a captain in charge, a captain whose personal valour set him apart from other players. The crowds at the matches sensed that they were experiencing something special, that O'Malley was whetting their appetites for a special result.

Michelle knew that something was wrong. It had been clear to her for a long time that Con, underneath his vibrant exterior, was not the man he used to be. She knew that he liked a flutter. She saw no harm in it, but there were important indicators that things were awry. Money was overtight. He lost his temper when she began to complain about the bills that never got paid, the evenings out that no longer happened. She thought that perhaps he was ill and urged him to see the doctor. He went eventually, needing to get her off his back and the doctor pronounced him fit and well. He was a trifle run down perhaps, but there was nothing to worry about. Michelle heard the verdict in silence, not entirely satisfied but unable to undermine the result.

Con suffered in silence. His gambling was a secret which had to be kept. His bets had become bigger and more foolhardy as he strove to recover his losses but he could not confide in anyone, least of all his wife. Michelle's parents had brought her up strictly. Her father liked a jar or two but that was the extent of his waywardness. They were thrifty good living people who lived for their daughter. She was their only child and they had lavished everything on her as she grew up. They had initially approved of her choice of husband, and although they had wondered at the apparent shortage of money over the last year or so, had not changed their opinions. Con O'Malley was a decent man who loved his wife and family, worked hard at his job as a builder's foreman, and had never given them cause to regret Michelle's choice.

Con knew that he enjoyed a lot of esteem. Much of his public persona, in fact virtually all of it, was due to his prowess on the football field, but he had never willingly deprived his family of their rightful share of the good things of life. His friends and relations relished his success and saw his care of Michelle and the children as an extension of his integrity, both as a sportsman and as a decent family man. His gambling was a dark secret shared by only a few. To the vast majority of his associates and the world at large, Con O'Malley was an open homespun hero, who could deliver great football and who had the added back up of a loving and admiring family.

PRIDE

Con brought Cian to the junior matches, standing on the sidelines with his son on his shoulders, or firmly clasping the small confident hand that clung to his own. Cian would be Con's immediate successor. Someday he too would captain the county team, score great goals, carrying on a family tradition. And there was tradition in the family. Con's father had been a footballer, and had captained the county team for a couple of seasons. Family lore had it that his grandfather too had been a stalwart of Stoneyford Gaels in the far off days when the Gaelic Athletic Association was an infant, and had yet to capture the imagination and backing of the country.

There was a faded photograph at home of a Gaels team in the 1920s, his grandfather sitting in the second row, wearing old fashioned long shorts, a wide grin on his face frozen by the camera. Con had a tradition in football. His sons would carry it on. He saw it as his duty to foster the same love of the game in Cian and Cormac as his own father had done with him. Footballers came in all shapes, good, bad and indifferent. The best were soon identified, and rose to the top. Con O'Malley had reached the top, he had stayed there for six or seven seasons and he was determined that when he finally left the game, people would remember him for the things he had achieved, for the glory he had brought to his club, and the lustre he had conferred on the game itself. Men like Con O'Malley were icons. They shared in the adulation of their supporters but they carried heavy burdens of contribution and performance as compensation for their glory.

Evan Jordan's demands weighed heavily on Con's mind. He cursed himself for his folly, for his recklessness, for the destitution which his habit was forcing upon him. But it was too late. Even if at this late stage he conquered his addiction, the damage was done. He had a mountainous debt and there were no other solutions in sight. Jordan had demanded his price. There was no way out. Con would have to comply no matter how great a risk this imposed. He was proud of his record in the game, proud of his position as captain for several successive seasons. He was proud too of his family. He loved his wife and he loved his sons, but he had been cursed with a vice from which there was no escape.

The gambler's innate and self cherished belief that he was winner, that the big scoop was only one bet away had sustained him in his folly for a long time now. But with a deep sense of foreboding he recognized that the end was approaching. He would obey Evan Jordan or face the consequences. If he failed to deliver at the match, Jordan's men would hunt him down. If he complied and actively threw the game, his reputation would be destroyed. He would be branded a cheat. The people who had once shouted his name from the sidelines would turn on him, cursing his furtive attempts to deprive their team of victory. He would have finally broken the rules that had sustained him throughout his playing life.

There was no doubt in Con's mind that if he went down the road mapped out by Jordan, people would see him for what he was. The bookie's stand on the match result was well known. It had been the talking point of the county for weeks. A fortune would be won and lost. If the result hinged on the legitimate turn of play well and good, but if there was any suggestion of malingering or crookedness by any one on the Stoneyford team, there would be calls for retribution. The Stoneyford supporters could live with defeat. There was no way, however, that they would tolerate any kind of fix which deprived them of rightful victory.

It was three days before the match when Jordan sought Con out again. He was waiting for the footballer when Con clocked off the site. The building workers streamed off towards the town and Con was about to get into his car and follow them when the bookie came up beside him. Both of them were big men, Jordan was a good ten years older, and Con would have been more than a match for him at any time. But Jordan didn't do his own enforcement. He had a team of thugs for that, hard vicious men who could be bought for small money and who would perpetrate whatever violence was necessary.

The bookie faced up to Con, confident of his control, his superiority, determined that he would get his way with the footballer. Money was everything to Evan Jordan. Like Con he was a gambler, or he wouldn't have been in the bookmaking business but he was a gambler who continually shortened the odds in his favour. He would make a lot of money if the match result went his way. Everything possible would be done to ensure that it did.

Jordan was certain that he was in control, but this encounter with Con was a form of reassurance. The football captain had been given his instructions. Jordan wanted to make sure that Con was clear in his mind about the role he was to play in the match.

"You know what has to be done," Jordan told Con. "Whatever happens, Stoneyford is to lose. I don't care how you do it, just make sure it works out. Remember," he added ingratiatingly, "you stand to gain a lot from this. You're into me for a lot of money. You'll be back on an even keel if the match goes our way. Remember that. You stand to gain a lot but you could lose a lot as well if you don't follow instructions."

Con said nothing. He wanted to smash his fist into the bookie's face, but there was no point. Violence at this stage would solve nothing. The bookie would send his henchmen to exact a brutal revenge. He would be out of the game, and the game itself was Con's life. To miss out for any reason was unthinkable.

"I know what you want," he said bitterly and turned away.

Jordan stood for a few moments, then satisfied, walked back to his car. Con O'Malley was a cowed man, he told himself. He would obey his instructions. The revenues from the county's gambling were as good as in Jordan's hands.

The days in the run-up to the match were a nightmare for Con O'Malley. He didn't sleep and was uncharacteristically bad tempered. Michelle put it down to pre match nerves and Con said nothing to change her opinion. He was drained, worn out, in no condition to play in a tough county cup final which would take every ounce of energy and concentration to bring to a fitting conclusion. Only this time the outcome would not be the one the fans had hoped for. Con O'Malley, their hero, their champion on so many occasions, was about to engage in the most deceitful action of his heady football career.

The final was usual was to be played on Sunday afternoon. They had a workout on the Friday. Con took part in a desultory sort of way but no one seemed to notice anything unusual. Everyone was preoccupied with their own problems, last minute sprains and strains, pre match nerves, all the issues which affected footballers coming up to a big occasion. Con stayed at home on Saturday. He slept late and didn't get up until around one o'clock. Still Michelle noticed nothing out of the way.

In the afternoon he brought Cian and Cormac out into the garden and kicked a ball around. The kids engaged and pursued the ball with shrieks of pleasure and Con mesmerised them with some fancy footwork and soft shots at improvised goal posts. For a while he lost himself in this heart warming contact with his children. When they were happy he was happy and the worry of what he had to do the following afternoon was briefly cast aside.

Finally when the kids were tired out and could play no more he put the ball away and brought them inside for tea. They were on a high, bolstered by their father's involvement in their afternoon, happy and content in the warmth of a loving relationship. Con adored his kids. Their enthusiasm stirred some inner chord. He could not let them down. There was no way he could allow them to see him engage in any kind of despicable action. He made up his mind, come what may, Con would do his best to ensure that his team emerged victorious from the next day's game. Evan Jordan could do his worst. For Con O'Malley basking at that moment in the loving embrace of his family, there was no other choice. He would play to the utmost of his ability. The outcome of the match would depend on the run of play. Con would do nothing to throw away his team's chances of victory.

Now that his decision was made, Con threw off the burden which he had been carrying. He went to the football ground the following day steeled with resolve. This might well be his last game. Evan Jordan might leave him a cripple, but he would have been honest with his team mates, with his family and with himself. This game would be the hallmark of his career. No one would know what he was undertaking. Afterwards his secret might come out. He would always be a gambler, but from now on he would be a gambler whose addiction could be controlled, put into a box. He would have faced down adversity, and emerged with his sportsman's reputation intact.

The game was hard fought. The run of play rolled backwards and forwards over the pitch and for most of the first half there was nothing between the teams. Con played at the top of his form and his team mates responded. They made the effort and just before the half time whistle blew a goal came their way. Con had not contributed directly. The effort had come from the far side of the pitch and was the result of a long low kick to the net by one of the other forwards.

As they trooped off to the dressing room Con saw Evan Jordan sitting high up in the stand. He smiled grimly to himself. The bookie could sit here as long as he liked. The outcome of the game would depend solely on the pressure and ability of the opposing teams. Con O'Malley might be heavily in debt, Jordan might think he had him in his grasp, but Con would do nothing to ensure that his team went down. It might well be that the result would have nothing at all to do with Con's own performance. Already the first goal had come off someone else's boot. The match would be won or lost on genuine effort. If the result went Jordan's way, so be it. Con O'Malley would not have been the cause of his team's downfall.

The second half saw a resurgence by the opposing team. Several times Con was called upon to even things up, to push the play into the opposite end of the pitch. It was a tough match. Neither side was needlessly giving ground and every yard of play was keenly contested. Eventually the opposition got a goal and with the score at a draw and only seven minutes left until the full time whistle blew, Con knew that victory would be down to him. A draw would not please Evan Jordan, but unless Stoneyford let something in at this late stage, the bookie's coup was already in the balance. Con made up his mind. He would destroy the bookie's chances altogether. Stoneyford would come out victorious and Jordan would have to take his beating.

An opportunity came his way almost immediately. There was a piece of heavy tackling and Stoneyford were given a free kick. Con took it and sent the ball up the pitch, high above the players heads. Stoneyford surged forward in pursuit. Con was in the vanguard. The ball came across to him, only one of the opposing team behind it. Con connected, got his boot behind the ball, and sent it into the net. Moments later the whistle blew. The Stoneyford supporters erupted. The cup was theirs, their team and its captain had made a Trojan effort. It was a match and a result which would be talked over in the pubs for weeks ahead.

PRIDE

Con followed his team mates into the dressing room and stole a glance up at the stand to where Jordan was sitting. He was too far away to see the expression on the bookie's face but his body language said it all. Con showered and changed in a thoughtful frame of mind, barely acknowledging the plaudits of the other players. The time of reckoning had still to come.

Jordan was waiting for him outside the ground. Con got into his own car and drove off, but not towards his home. He led the way out into the countryside. Jordan followed. The bookie was alone and Con knew that he was safe enough for the moment. Jordan was a big man, but he was no match for the footballer, his physique hardened not just by his efforts on the pitch, but by his daily work. The building sites made a man tough too. Con O'Malley was a rough hewn man who could hold his own against any adversary. He was sure that he would be able to successfully take on a couple of Jordan's men. The bookie, however, would send more than this. Three or four would be dispatched to teach Con O'Malley a lesson.

In the mean time Jordan was following Con. The footballer wondered why he came on his own and then decided that the bookie wanted the satisfaction of making personal threats, of promised vengeance and retaliation. Con pulled up the car on a quiet stretch of road and got out. Jordan stopped as well. There was no one in sight. He walked to the bookie's car and pulled open the door on the driver's side. Jordan was suddenly alarmed. This wasn't what he had expected. Con hauled him out of the car and smashed a fist into the bookie's face. He hammered again and again until the bookie was unconscious. Then he flung Jordan back into his car and walked away.

Jordan's men might come around later, but for the moment Con O'Malley had shown that he was not a man to be trifled with. He was as tough as Jordan or any of his men and he could look after himself. Jordan had once warned the footballer about the consequences of a refusal to carry out his demands. Now Con O'Malley had issued his own warning. Jordan was vulnerable. O'Malley would come for him when his men were not around. He had shown the bookie what he was capable of. Con O'Malley might be a gambler, but he was no weakling. Men who were heroes on the football field knew how to look after themselves. They could play any game, inside and outside the rules.

Remorse

The jury filed slowly back into their seats, eight men and four women. They were quiet, subdued. One man looked directly across the floor of the court at him, a half grimace on his face. The others avoided eye contact and either looked downwards or up at the judge.

Mallon glanced at his barrister looking for reassurance but the lawyer was looking fixedly at a sheaf of papers on the table in front of him. He felt a moment of panic. Already before the verdict had been announced he knew what the jury were going to say. Guilty! It wasn't a surprise. The evidence had been against him from the start. It was a horrific tale. Three people, a woman and two children had been killed in the crash. The police had breathalised Mallon and he had been found to be well over the limit. There were no mitigating circumstances, unless the traditional exonerating excuse of drink taken was advanced in mitigation. But being drunk had been one of the lesser charges, while manslaughter resulting in the deaths of three people had been the headline accusation.

Mallon had realized from the outset that he would go to prison once he had sobered up in the police cell and realized the enormity of what he had done. He had killed three people, two of them children. It was a nightmare and one from which there was no escape.

The woman's husband had been in court every day, a man bereft of his family, suffering incredible pain. He had sat there quietly, ashen, a look of steely determination on his face. He wanted to see justice done. He wanted to see Mallon sentenced. It was part of his therapy, a small measure of consolation for his pain.

Mallon too had pain, but it was a different kind. He was afraid, suffering cold frozen feelings of apprehension about what lay ahead. Yet there was some hope as well. Perhaps things were not as black as they looked. Perhaps he would get a short sentence, perhaps it would even be suspended. But inside he knew that this was not going to happen. His barrister had been able to say little in mitigation. His client had been drunk in charge and he had wiped out a mother and her two children. The law would take its course. The penalty would be severe. Everyone in court knew it. Mallon was clutching at straws when he tried to fleetingly convince himself that there would be any other outcome.

He stood up when the judge called out his name. There was a short preamble before he reached the hard core of his speech, the sentence. Mallon had been guilty of gross negligence he told him. He had deliberately chosen to drive while drunk. He had taken lives, young lives, and he must serve seven years for manslaughter, plus three years for driving while drunk, the sentences to run concurrently.

Mallon fell back on the bench behind him and wiped tears from his eyes. He must keep control. He mustn't let anyone see that he was stricken. There was a brief silence in the court, then scraping of feet and rising bodies as the judge left the chamber. The sound of voices soon filled the room as people debated the result. Mallon's barrister looked at him sympathetically, then gathered up his papers and made his way towards the back of the court and the exit. A prison guard touched Mallon on the shoulder and led him from the dock. Handcuffs and a short chain secured him to the guard and he was pushed forward into the departing sightseers.

Outside a television camera recorded his brief walk to the prison van. No one else was interested now. The sight of convicted men being led away in chains was commonplace. The rest of the world went about its business. Only those from whom justice sought reparation felt the pain and injury of those first few moments of lost liberty.

208

REMORSE

The trip to the prison was uneventful. There were two other prisoners in the van, all of them manacled and sitting beside escorting prison officers. Mallon wondered briefly why so much manpower was needed. It was unlikely that there would be any attempt at escape. The next few hours passed in a haze. He showered and was examined by the prison doctor and assigned to a three bunk cell. Incarceration had begun.

Mallon settled in over the next few weeks. He had an interview with a deputy prison governor who advised him succinctly to keep to the rules, the prison chaplain made himself known and Mallon had a session with his solicitor. The lawyer was not encouraging about an appeal. The crime had been horrendous, there were no real grounds for going back into court, and there was always the possibility that his sentence could be increased. He should not forget, the lawyer advised him sternly, that two children and their mother were dead. There was an element of righteousness in the lawyer's words as if he agreed with the penalty that had been imposed. For a moment Mallon reflected with some bitterness that with people like this on his side he had little real chance of being acquitted.

Reluctantly Mallon agreed with the lawyer's conclusions about an appeal and the man left. It was the last time that he would come to see him. He had no other business with the prisoner and legal aid did not cover idle social calls. Mallon went back to his cell far from reconciled to his lot but relieved that a decision had been reached. The lawyer had advised him that if he kept his nose clean in jail he would be eligible for parole when half his sentence had been served. Three and a half years, after all, was not that long. They would pass and Mallon could then resume life on the outside, marked perhaps by his experience but nonetheless free to resume some kind of normal life.

He had been in prison for more than two months when he had

his first visitor. At first Mallon did not recognize the name. He had the option of choosing and refusing visitors and he was tempted to decline the visit. Then when he realized who wanted to see him he agreed. Sean Hughes was the husband and father whom he had so cruelly deprived of his family. Mallon was nervous and hesitant about his caller. They sat opposite each other along the wide benches and low separating partition the height of a table tennis net that prevented things being passed from visitor to inmate. The practice was that visitors left their parcels at the point of entry and they were delivered later to the cells. Sean Hughes apparently had brought nothing. Mallon was not surprised. He expected nothing. This man surely was not a visitor with any feeling of goodwill towards the man he had come to see.

Mallon waited expectantly. He was prepared for some sort of abuse, of condemnation, but his visitor was mild and soft spoken. His face was lined with tiredness and it was clear that even though two years had passed since his family were killed he had not got over the impact of that terrible event.

Sean Hughes was clear and succinct. He had come with a purpose. He wanted to see what kind of man had killed his family, to find out whether there was any real remorse, or whether Mallon was really the cold unmoved individual he had appeared to be in court.

"I want to get to know you," Hughes said quietly. "I want to find out what kind of man you are. I want to know if I can forgive you or whether I will hate you for the rest of my life."

Mallon was silent. This softly spoken man was just as much a victim of that terrible event as his wife and children. Mallon might be in jail but the day would come when he would be released, his time served, the penalty which the state demanded for his crime expiated. But Sean Hughes had a lifetime sentence. His wounds would last for ever. There would be no healing, no relief, each day that passed would be visited by the relentless torment of having lost those who were most dear to him.

Mallon was irritated. What did this man want. Why had he come to plague him. Did he want to experience for himself the sight of his assailant behind bars. Did he want to experience revenge at first hand. Was this visit a method of tormenting the man who had brought so much desolation into his life.

Hughes evidently understood what was going through Mallon's mind.

"I hate you for what you did," his visitor said quietly. "But I don't want to live out my life with this hate. I want my own kind of freedom. I need to know that you are being punished, that you truly regret what you have done to me."

Mallon was lost for words. This speech was the last thing he expected. Hatred, venom, yes, but a quiet recitation of this man's search for reconciliation knocked him off balance. He was suspicious. Surely something else lurked behind his visitor's words. Surely there was a deeper purpose. Had he mapped out a special kind of vengeance.

That evening in his cell Mallon thought over his visitor's words. It was strange. If Mallon had been in Sean Hughes's place he would have been filled with hate, with a desire to hurt the perpetrator of his misery as much as possible. But here was this quiet man coming to see him in prison, offering if not forgiveness exactly some kind of curious friendship.

At the end of the trial the newspapers had said that Mallon was cold, unemotional, taking the verdict and sentence dispassionately. The media all too often rushed to their own kind of judgment, were more demanding, more denunciatory in their outbursts than the verdicts of the courts. Mallon had read the reports angrily. He had been given a considerable number of column inches. The case with its tragic overtones had come at a time when other news was scarce and the newspapers, the tabloids in particular had the space and the inclination to run riot. They loved a villain, particularly a villain who could not hit back. This was a man who had killed two little girls. He had to be excoriated. The public, the red top readers in particular, demanded it. Mallon threw the papers aside and cursed them for their eviscerating prose. They knew nothing about him. All they were doing was revelling in the anguish not just of the man who had been condemned but of the family who had suffered.

Later, however, he reflected on what they had said. He was a cold man. He had taken his sentencing without any indication of his inner feelings. But what were his inner feelings. He had steeled himself for the verdict, determined that he would not show any weakness. Was this not the brave thing to do. To be stalwart, to be firm in adversity. He was sorry for what he had done, but this did not mean that he had to become a crying abject wreck of a man, seeking absolution, forgiveness. Being in jail was a tough call, but Mallon believed that he could meet the challenges that it threw up.

Mallon would survive by being cold, hard, unaffected by his surroundings, the discipline, the control, the inability to make his own decisions. But there was one decision that Mallon could make. He would not let his circumstances break him. If this meant being aloof, impregnable, lacking in feeling or consideration for others, then so be it. Everyone in jail had to survive in his own way. Everyone had to deal with the demons which being locked in a cage conjured up. Mallon was a survivor. He would come out of prison unscathed. He had killed people but he would not carry any open wounds from the encounter.

REMORSE

Sean Hughes came again a few weeks later. This time Mallon went to see him in the visitors' hall with less trepidation but some measure of curiosity. What did Hughes expect to gain from these encounters. Was he such a pathetic man that he could only draw consolation from these visits with the man who was responsible for his hurt. Surely Hughes could not really want to be his friend. Mallon wondered if the man had become unbalanced, if he needed some kind of therapy which in some perverted way he thought that Mallon could provide. But there was no sign of anguish or disturbance in his visitor's appearance. He was quiet and normal, his colour was better than on the first visit. Mallon supposed that going into a prison for whatever purpose was an unpleasant experience. Hughes might have been nervous on that occasion, uncertain of his reception, perhaps even unclear about what he was attempting to do.

That was the kernel of the issue. What was Hughes attempting to do. Mallon wondered if he would try to bring some religious experience to bear on their conversation, perhaps that was his motivation, but the man did not appear to be interested in saving his soul. He said no prayers nor made any references to God. Mallon settled down to listen and perhaps to gain some understanding of what these visits were all about.

"You are wondering why I've come again," was Sean Hughes' opening remark.

Mallon nodded silently.

"As I said before, I want to get to know you," Hughes went on. "We share a great deal. Our lives have touched. The effect of that will last for ever."

"You're sick," Mallon burst out. "Why do you keep coming here. We can never be friends. What do you want."

213

"No" Hughes answered. "We can never be friends. But I need to know you and I want you to know me. We can be of some solace to each other."

"I don't want any solace," Mallon retorted. "I can deal with my own problems. You should look out for yourself."

"That's exactly what I'm doing," Hughes replied. "It is important for me to come here. I need to know everything about you, your thoughts, your emotions, how you deal with the fact that you are a murderer."

There was an unexpected tone of menace in Hughes' last words.

Mallon stiffened. For the first time he had sensed anger in his visitor. For the first time he thought that he detected an underlying motive for these visits. Did Hughes intend to attack him. Would he bring in a weapon. Could this be the answer. Hughes was a madman driven insane by his terrible loss. He was out to exact a bloody revenge.

Mallon was unafraid. He was physically strong and he would be able to overpower his smaller, slighter opponent.

Yes, he told himself. This was the answer. Hughes would come several times to allay suspicion, to become a familiar figure to the prison staff, to even convince Mallon himself that he meant no harm. Then one day he would strike. It was unlikely that he would bring in a gun. A knife was the likely weapon. It could be easily concealed. There were no body searches of visitors. This wasn't a subversive prison. Women's handbags were cursorily examined, but unless male visitors were obviously carrying some undeclared object, they would never be challenged.

The staff were always on the lookout for drugs, of course, but they had their targets. Drugs were freely available within the prison and the users were easily identified. Some were on methadone treatment but for the most part the prison officers let things go. Occasionally the governor would decide on cell searches and there would be a clamp down but eventually the screws eased up and life got on as before. Mallon wasn't a drugs user and had no intention of becoming one. He intended to be strong during his incarceration. On the outside alcohol had been his disease but in here temptation was removed. There was no drink and he had ceased to feel the hunger. No, Mallon was stronger inside the jail than he had been on the outside.

Weaker men could go down the drugs route or even succumb to the need for legitimate prescribed tranquilisers, but Mallon was not like these people. He could survive without any artificial stimulants or sessions with the prison psychiatrists. But perhaps Hughes intended to go down this route. Perhaps he was more devious than Mallon gave him credit for. Perhaps he intended to supply Mallon with drugs, to turn him into a dependant supplicating wreck of a man. Mallon smiled grimly to himself. That would be a subtle and effective form of revenge. Mallon a drug addict would be forever destroyed. An addiction would last well beyond his prison years.

Yes that was an option for this strange quiet visitor who professed his need for ongoing contact with the man who had done him such great harm. If Mallon were in Hughes' place he might go down this road. There was less risk. It was a cruel and satisfying form of revenge, long drawn out and offering the opportunity for a lengthy savouring of the process.

But Hughes had brought nothing with him. He made no adversarial moves, only that tinge of menace in his voice had alerted Mallon to the fact that there was anger under the veneer of quiet compassion which this man exuded.

215

"I don't want you to come again," Mallon told him deciding that these encounters had to stop. He didn't know what to make of this man but he wasn't going to take any further chances. "I won't see you again. I'll tell the prison. You won't get in. I have the right to refuse to see visitors."

Hughes smiled knowingly.

"You have no one else," he said. "I've made enquiries. You have no family and your friends have given up on you. They were only bar-room buddies, anyway," he went on. "People like that have no compassion, they don't know how to bond with people. They don't care about you. You've gone out of their lives. You have no one, only me. I'm the only person in the world taking any interest in you."

Mallon sat back in his chair suddenly struck by the brutal truth of what his visitor was saying. There was no one else. No one came to see him apart from this strange quiet man with his curious need to befriend the drunk who had destroyed his life.

"I suppose you're right in what you say," Mallon said, slowly acquiescing to the truth to the point that the visitor had made. He was alone. There was no one. For a fleeting moment Mallon felt lost, victimized, then he got a grip on himself.

"I can live without anyone," he said confidently. "I don't need you to come and see me. I will get through this on my own. Leave me alone. Don't come back."

Hughes was silent for a moment or two.

"That's your decision," he said eventually. "I can't force you to see me, but I think you should. I am a link with the outside world. I will be frank with you. I have come to see you for my own reasons but you are getting something out of my visits as well."

216

"I don't know what you want," Mallon said angrily. "I don't understand you. You're some sort of nut, coming here like this. I killed your family. Don't you understand that."

"You did indeed," Hughes responded. "I shall never forget what you did. I will carry the wounds for the rest of my life. You have destroyed me and I shall do the same to you."

With that Hughes got up and left. Mallon sat for a few moments waiting for the officer to bring him back to his cell. Finally he had got an admission from his visitor. He came with a purpose and that purpose was revenge. Mallon couldn't understand how he proposed to achieve his aims. Talking surely would not accomplish anything.

A week later Hughes came to the prison again. Mallon was baffled, but despite his previous stance and warning to Hughes that he would not see him, he agreed to do so.

"This is the last time I'm going to see you," he told his visitor flatly.

Hughes smiled and brought a rolled up sheet from his inside pocket. He pushed it over the partition to Mallon. The warder on duty missed the move. Mallon spread the sheet out on the table in front of him. It was a child's painting, a family outside their house. Father, mother and two small children. A whisp of smoke rose from the red chimney pot. The painting was clumsily done, a child's expression of love and intimacy, and the waterpaint had been smeared as it was applied, but it undoubtedly conveyed a message.

"Our youngest daughter did that two days before you killed her," Hughes said. "We were a family and now we are nothing. They have gone and this is all that is left behind."

He leaned forward and looked directly into Mallon's eyes.

"I want you to have this," he said. "I want you to have this memento of what you have done. I want you to keep it in your cell and look at it. You never knew my children but you will have this to remind you of them."

Mallon was strangely touched. For a moment his hard man veneer was penetrated. But he regained his composure almost immediately. What did this man hope to achieve by giving him his child's legacy. Hughes smiled his quiet curious smile and nodded as if agreeing with Mallon's unspoken thought.

He leaned forward again.

"I will break you" he said without emphasis. "Be sure of that. I'm getting there."

Mallon laughed harshly. He was tempted to hand the painting back but the warder was watching and instead he rolled it up and held on to it.

"You're getting nowhere with me," he said. "This game is a load of nonsense. I know what you're trying to do. You want to undermine me, see me break down and beg for forgiveness. Well that's not going to happen. I'm sorry for what happened, I've told you that already, but I intend to put it all behind me. I will get out of here in due course and I will have my life back again."

His visitor smiled again.

"I'm winning," he said. You don't realise it but you're going down. It won't be long now."

Mallon decided that he had heard enough. He got up and signaled to the warder. He looked back as he left the visitors' hall. Hughes was still seating at the bench, still smiling. He raised a hand and waved it, a final derisive farewell.

218

REMORSE

It was over, Mallon decided as he walked along the landing on the way back to his cell. He definitely wouldn't see Hughes again. The man was clearly unhinged. Grief had unbalanced him.

He lay down on his bunk and unrolled the painting again. Despite the fact that it was clumsy, unskilled, scrawled across the page, it was strangely compelling. Mallon wondered what Hughes had hoped to achieve by giving it to him. Surely it had to be a valued possession, a tangible link with the family he had lost.

Exasperated he flung it down and then picked it up again. He had some sellotape in his locker and smoothing the furled page out stuck it to the wall. He lay back on his bunk and stared at it for a long time. There was something compelling about its smeared symmetry.

He lay back and thought about the accident. It was the first time since he trial that he had really confronted the issue. It was part of his strong willed approach to the event to ignore the detail, to drive from his mind the drunken haze of the crash itself, the few days in hospital, the police questions, the awful reality that he would go to prison. Now that he was locked up with a determined period to his incarceration he felt more resigned. At least there was a limit to his punishment. One day he would be free and he would have survived.

Mallon's thoughts returned again to his visitor. What had driven Sean Hughes to come to the jail and confront him on three different occasions. What had he to gain. Did he relish the sight of Mallon as a prisoner. Was he getting some form of perverted satisfaction from the sight of a locked up man, his freedom taken away in expiation of his crime.

Mallon was certain that Sean Hughes derived considerable satisfaction from his plight. Hughes wouldn't have been human otherwise, but always there had been something more to him. Hughes was in search of a greater degree of vengeance, but Mallon didn't understand his approach. A quiet baiting of a man under lock and key could only provide satisfaction for a limited time, but Hughes was so certain that there was more to be gained. 'I'm winning,' he had said. 'You're going down.'

What was he winning. How was he winning. Mallon was impregnable, had forced himself to deal with the crisis in his life. There was no way that Hughes could undo him.

He glanced at the child's painting taped to the cell wall. Suddenly the full import of what Sean Hughes had said struck home. He was terribly alone. The man whom he had so cruelly wronged was his only visitor. No one else cared. Unbidden tears came to Mallon's eyes. He jumped up and tore down the picture from the wall. There was an accusation there, a wrathful presence that shattered his resolve and overcame all his strength. The façade that he had built around himself was shattered. He was a man alone, in terrible circumstances, a man who had committed the most awful crime of all, the destruction and slaughter of two young children and their mother. The enormity of his crime overwhelmed him. His resolve was struck down, his willpower eroded. Mallon was no longer strong and invincible. His armour had been pierced, all his defence mechanisms destroyed.

The warders found Mallon hunched up in his bunk the following morning, tears still streaming down his face. They knew that Mallon had cracked and were not surprised. Things happened to even the strongest men in jail. They took him out of his cell and led him to the infirmary. The doctors would take over now, there would be a long regime of counseling and medication as they tried to repair a broken man. Sean Hughes had got his revenge.